GUNHAWKS

Puzzled, Calem lifted his head. Suddenly a running man appeared close by. Calem jerked up his gun but didn't fire. The Fifty-four man ran with jerky steps, eyes stretched wide, a growing stain of crimson on his shirt.

He was a running dead man.

They heard the man crash down, then Crocker found the nerve to bob his head up and take a look. He almost fell back down, his eyes stretched wide in amazement.

"It's Brazos and Benedict, Curly!" he gasped. "They're up on the ridge!"

As an astounded Curly Calem lifted his head, a cry of pain sounded from close by. The Anvil man had a glimpse of the towering Ram Brand staggering away favoring his left leg. Lead howled down from above and Brazos' booming voice sounded above the guns.

"Ride out, Fifty-four, or we'll bury the bunch of you!"

GUNHAWKS ON THE LOOSE

★ E. JEFFERSON CLAY ★

*Published through
arrangement with
Piccadilly Publishing*

Gunhawks on the Loose was originally published in the 1970s. Though certain characterizations and slang may be objectionable to contemporary readers, the text has not been edited from the original edition to preserve the integrity of the author's words.

Series editor: Ben Bridges, Piccadilly Publishing

Series editor: Rich Harvey, Bold Venture Press

Bold Venture Press paperback edition.
Available in electronic editions from Piccadilly Publishing.
Published through arrangement with Piccadilly Publishing.

Originally published 1975 in Australia by Cleveland Publishing Co. Pty, Ltd.

This is a work of fiction. Though some characters and locales may have their basis in history, the events and characters depicted herein are fictitious.

GUNHAWKS
ON THE
LOOSE

1

Day of the Fast Guns

CASS TUCKER was the first to see the riders. She was busy making starch from potato water in the kitchen of the Fifty-four ranch house when she happened to look out the window and saw them coming in.

They were a long way off, perhaps two miles, maybe more, and they were like two shimmering blobs against the yellow grass. Cass watched them for some minutes, her thin body relaxed and her brows drawn together in a frown. Now and then she pushed two fingers at her pale hair where perspiration made it cling to her cheeks. The rippling heat played tricks with the riders, moving them up and down like leaves on a creek, but at the end of five minutes they seemed to be no closer to Fifty-four headquarters.

Cass thought of telling her father, but in this heat it scarcely seemed worth it. In any case, if the men on the verandah hadn't seen the riders they would soon. She looked at the old Halliday wind pump beyond the horse corrals. Joe Tucker had ordered the pump from Denver five years ago, when he believed the drovers from the south would pass through the valley every year on their way to Sheridan. Water and whisky were important to drovers, and Joe Tucker had set up a plank bar and a wind pump here at the house to supply both—at a price. But the drovers had come one year and that was all. A spur off the main line at Tackville had given the cattlemen a shipping point fifty miles closer than Sheridan. The Tuckers and the wind pump had stayed on, and the Fifty-four Ranch had grown up around them. Cass often believed her father would have been better off to take his pump and whisky supply somewhere else instead of staying on to raise beef. For one thing, it would have saved a lot of lives …

The girl had almost forgotten the two riders when young Billy Tanner came running in to take the old field glasses down from their hook above the fireplace.

"Riders comin' in, Miss Cass," he grinned in his wild way as he trotted out. "Your pa reckons it might be them fellers from Clanton Gulch."

Cass felt her stomach knot as she went to the window. Her father and the men now stood in the yard staring west. She caught a glimpse of her father's smiling face as he lowered the glasses. Then the two horsemen came in. Both were fair headed and each wore double guns.

The girl pressed her hands against her stomach and sank down to the old kitchen chair with the peeling lemon paint. She felt she was going to be ill. Trouble was coming; she knew it in the awful dryness of her throat and the wild hammering of her heart. Pa had threatened to bring in professional guns following the last clash with the Anvil Ranch, and the two strangers out there under the brassy sun had the look of men who made their living through dealing out death.

Cass closed her eyes and rested her forehead against the cool, damp porcelain of the sink, trying to shut her mind to what was happening. She had already seen too much violence and bloodshed in her father's feud with Burk Kincaid.

She didn't think she could take any more.

***

It had all been Hank Brazos' fault.

Duke Benedict was quite certain of this in his own mind as he sat in his cell at the Sheridan jailhouse late that afternoon flicking playing cards at his upturned hat.

Brazos could have ignored the blacksmith's sarcastic remarks about Texas. But being a Texan with a Texan's ridiculous pride, he hadn't.

It had happened last night in the Paylode Saloon. Duke Benedict and Hank Brazos, on the drift and looking for work, had arrived in Sheridan just on sundown. Their steps had led them automatically to the town's biggest saloon. The Paylode's whisky was good and the girls were passably pretty. In no time at all Duke Benedict was seated behind a full house, aces up, with a large pot in the center of the table and a bright-eyed blonde named Molly McQuade seeing that his bourbon glass was kept filled. The picture of a contented man was Duke Benedict, what with the chance of a winning night coming up to delay the specter of "work."

Then it happened. The burly 'smith at the bar suddenly decided in a loud voice that Texans walked too tall. As Hank Brazos stood six-three in his stockinged feet, this could have been interpreted as nothing worse than an envious observation from a thick-headed blacksmith who was some six inches shorter.

Soaking up the beer and boasting about his trail hound to the barkeep, Brazos, after a long, slow look at the black-bearded 'smith, had seemed ready to let it go at that.

Then blacksmith Hutch Stovey, who had been kicked out of the Lone Star State years ago after crippling a Texas Ranger in a roughhouse brawl, announced loud and clear that there was only one kind of good Texan.

Ugly Hutch hadn't needed to go into detail as to precisely what kind of Texan he meant. Everybody understood immediately, including the towering newcomer in the faded purple shirt who believed that if a man lived right and said his prayers regularly, when he died he would be sent to Texas.

The fight was short and spectacular. Brazos hit Stovey three times, once for Texas, once for Sam Houston, and the third out of simple annoyance that a man could be so uncivil to a peace-loving stranger like himself.

So far so good. The thud of the blacksmith's heavy body as he measured his length on the floor prompted nothing more from Benedict than a casual glance before he murmured, "Your five and up five."

Then the skinny, hot-eyed kid bought in. He wore a tied-down six-shooter, was full of rye whisky and indignation, and saw in the situation a chance to acquire respect that had been too long denied him. Staggering from his chair in the corner, he shouted at Brazos and pulled his gun.

Duke Benedict acted without thinking. He dropped his winning hand, drew with the fluent action of the true gun hand, and fired.

His aim had never been better. The six-gun spun from the kid's hand, its cylinder burst open by the impact of the bullet. The kid was still hopping around, howling and clutching his jarred wrist, when the batwings burst open and the fat sheriff came in at a trot.

The kid was the sheriff's nephew.

What had followed was as unfortunate a situation as Duke Benedict had ever been involved in. The sheriff didn't permit gunplay in his town. There had been far too much shooting going on around Keogh County of late, and the lawman was damned if he was going to let a pair of strangers ride in and start shooting up the place.

Benedict was eminently reasonable as he tried to convince the sheriff that no one had "shot up the place." What had happened, he explained soberly, was that there had been a small difference of opinion between his partner and the blacksmith that certainly didn't warrant a "pimply-faced pipsqueak" resorting to gunplay.

It was then and there that they discovered the "pipsqueak" was the sheriff's nephew. Inside of ten minutes they found themselves occupying separate cells at the jailhouse. It didn't help much to learn later from the deputy that the sheriff had taken his nephew into the barn and had beaten the hell out of him with a saddle girth. All that really mattered was that they were in jail with a fifty-dollar fine hanging over their heads for disturbing the peace.

And it was all Hank Brazos' fault, Duke Benedict thought as he flicked the last card. Fifty pasteboards were in the upturned black hat across the cell. He'd missed only twice. His hand and eye were still steady, despite the fact that his temper was worsening by the hour.

His mood was hardly improved when Brazos began to stroll up and down his cell blowing through the harmonica he wore on a rawhide cord around his neck. Johnny Reb's selection was *The Yellow Rose of Texas*.

Duke Benedict's gray eyes were cold as he leaned back on his hard bunk and took out his cigar case. There were times, he reflected, when a man needed a trail partner with a matchless knowledge of the wilds and a pair of ready fists. At such times, Hank Brazos could be tolerated. But there were other times—many of them—when travelling the West with the Texan was a painful ordeal.

Brazos played *The Yellow Rose of Texas* all the way through, then launched into *Remember San Jancento*. The drink-ruined bum in the cell across the corridor knew San Jancento. He got to his feet and started to sing. His voice was high and cracked and he kept time with his flap-soled boots. Encouraged by this interest, Brazos played even louder, conducted with his free hand and did a little Texas jig.

The big oaf was enjoying it, Benedict thought bitterly. Of course, he supposed, a jail cell would seem almost comfortable to one who had been reared in a Texas sod hut where goats grazed on the grassed roof. He would be happy here playing his fool harmonica and getting on first-name terms with his jailers, secure in the knowledge that Benedict would figure out a way to get them out of this mess. When it came to straight brainwork, responsibility inevitably rested on the well-tailored shoulders of Marmaduke Creighton Benedict the Third.

The handsome gambling man with the cigar set between his teeth, sighed deeply as he thought longingly of the great house in far-off Boston where he had grown up as the pampered son of one of the richest men on the Eastern seaboard. What had happened to that gracious, elegant way of life and the young man who had been tutored and trained to one day take over from his father?

Benedict knew the answer only too well. What had happened was the four years of hell they called the Civil War. Like so many others, Duke Benedict had ridden off to war to become a different man. He had come to look upon danger and adventure as the norm; Boston had grown too placid for him. The West beckoned, and Duke Benedict answered its exciting call. The West had not disappointed him. There was enough excitement and adventure to suit even the wildest spirit. Sighing again, Benedict turned his head at the sound of steps from the front office.

Sheriff Barney Rudkin loomed at the cell door. The sheriff of Sheridan's huge bulk was encased in a vast twill shirt and voluminous moleskin trousers.

The sheriff started to speak but couldn't make himself heard above the harmonica music and the vocalist. Rudkin took out his keys and slammed them hard against the bars. Brazos turned and immediately lowered the mouth organ with a grin.

"One more verse, Texas!" slurred red-faced Hyram Jolley from his cell.

"One more *peep* out of you could be your last, rumdum," the sheriff barked, and the drunk fell silent, his bottom lip sticking out petulantly.

"Just brightenin' things up a little, Sheriff," Brazos said amiably. "Supper time yet?"

The sheriff's response was a scowl. Then he turned back to Benedict and said, "Visitor to see you."

"Who? The governor with a pardon?" Benedict's tone was sarcastic. He supposed he could understand Rudkin's anxiety to keep things peaceable in his town, but this didn't make him warm to the man any.

"You talk awful sassy for somebody in your spot without the wherewithal to buy his way out, Benedict," the sheriff said. He glanced towards the archway that gave onto the office, then said importantly, "The man who wants to see you is Burk Kincaid."

"Is that name supposed to mean something to me?"

"It should. Mr. Kincaid is the richest man in Keogh County. He owns the Anvil Ranch."

"The Anvil!" Brazos said, impressed. He looked at Benedict as he got to his feet. "That's a really big outfit, Yank. Matter of fact, I was thinkin' we could go out there and see if they want a pair of hands."

Benedict winced. The prospect of ranch work might appeal to former cowboy Brazos, but not to a man of Benedict's special skills. He leaned against the bars and stared at Rudkin's big, meaty face.

"What does this man want with me?"

"Says he wants to talk," Rudkin replied. "Says he might be willin' to pay your fine."

Benedict's eyes narrowed. "Why should a stranger want to do that?"

"Never look a gift horse in the mouth, Benedict," Brazos said. "Send this here feller in, Sheriff. You can tell him there's one jailbird at least that's pinin' for a little free air."

"It's you he wants to see, Benedict," Rudkin said. "What will I tell him?"

Benedict shrugged. "Let him come in."

"Mebbe he's heard we're lookin' for work, Yank?" Brazos said as the sheriff trudged off. "Could be luck's runnin' our way at last."

Not at all sure that the luck involved in landing a ranch job would be good or bad, Duke Benedict gave no reply. He stood at the door puffing on his cheroot, his dark hair gleaming and his handsome face blank as the man came through the archway.

12

Burk Kincaid was a tall man with a carefully clipped moustache and keen eyes. He was also a man of direct and deliberate ways. After introducing himself and giving the prisoners a careful perusal, he got straight down to business. He needed two good hands on Anvil. If Benedict and Brazos were interested, he would pay their fines and start them off immediately. The wages would be eighty dollars a week each.

Until the cattleman mentioned the wages, Hank Brazos had been enthusiastic. But now he frowned, his blue eyes staring through the bars in puzzlement at the boss of Anvil.

"Eighty a week, Mr. Kincaid?" he breathed. "Glory, man. where we've been, punchers don't make that much in two months."

"With twenty men on my payroll, I'm well aware of the going rate for hands, Mr. Brazos," Kincaid said. "I'm not looking for cowpunchers."

"What *are* you looking for, Mr. Kincaid?" Benedict asked.

"Trouble-shooters."

Benedict let out his breath. "Do you mean gunfighters?"

"I mean what I say. You may or may not know, Mr. Benedict, that there has been trouble between the Anvil and Joe Tucker's Fifty-four Ranch. It's a difference of long standing, and recently it's grown worse. I won't go into all the details, but I heard today that the Fifty-four has hired two gunfighters, the Brand brothers from Clanton Gulch. As I can only interpret this as a deliberately aggressive action on Tucker's behalf, I have no option but to take counter measures to protect myself."

Benedict and Brazos exchanged a glance. Then Benedict said quietly:

"And what makes you believe we're the kind of men you need, Mr. Kincaid?"

"One of my men was at the Paylode last night when you had that run-in with Matt Baylor, the sheriff's nephew," Kincaid replied without hesitation. "Brad Cooley is one of my troubleshooters. He told me that you handled yourself commendably, and now, having met you, I'm convinced you're what I am looking for. Will you accept my offer?"

"No."

Both Brazos and Benedict replied together.

The rancher looked surprised. "But I don't understand. I'm not asking you to hire your guns in the strict sense. I'm simply looking for somebody with the ability to help me protect my life and property. You men obviously have that ability—"

"Sorry, Mr. Kincaid," Brazos cut him off. "Benedict and me ain't that kind. Sure, mebbe we know one end of a gun from the other, and mebbe the Yank here is rated mighty high in some places in the six-gun line. But we ain't guns-for-hire."

"That's how it is, Mr. Kincaid," Benedict confirmed. "In our experience, the hiring of guns in situations such as you describe almost invariably makes things worse. It's a generous offer, but we're simply not interested."

But Burk Kincaid was not the kind to give up easily, and despite their refusal, the rancher launched into a grim account of the conditions on his ranch, the violent intractability of Joe Tucker, and the cost the feud had already exacted in blood and men's lives.

The Anvil boss was a persuasive speaker, and though Benedict and Brazos found themselves sympathetic towards such an obviously honest man confronted by a big problem, they remained adamant. More than once during their partnership, they had found themselves drawn into such conflicts by circumstances, and they had always come to regret it.

Finally realizing he was making no headway, Kincaid took another tack. Could men in their position afford not to accept his offer? How would they pay their fines?

"That's just something we'll have to work out for ourselves," Benedict declared.

But Kincaid wouldn't admit defeat. They seemed like men of honor and integrity, he pointed out. Could they live with themselves if the Fifty-four's new gun hands were to cost more innocent lives on the Anvil? Could they just walk away from the situation, not caring?

The cattleman was making it hard to keep saying no, but they managed it until a girl called out from the office:

"Father? Are you nearly through?"

"My daughters," Kincaid sighed. "They are growing impat—" The rancher broke off abruptly, glancing sharply from one man to the other. Then he turned and said, "Sheriff, let the girls come through for a moment, will you?"

"Damn it, man," Benedict said testily, "it's bad enough to find oneself in a prison cell without suffering the added embarrassment of women witnessing his—"

He stopped talking as the two girls appeared. They were both quite young, the taller one plain and serious looking, but the other slim, petite and radiantly pretty. In their clean blue gingham and poke bonnets, they looked totally out of place in the cell-block as they stopped near their father and peered nervously through the bars at the prisoners.

"Mr. Benedict, Mr. Brazos," Kincaid murmured. "My daughters Sarah," he indicated the thin girl, "and Emma."

Sarah Kincaid nodded formally, but pretty Emma smiled and said, "How do you do, gentlemen?" Then she turned to her father. "It really is time we were heading home. It will be dark before we get there as it is."

But Kincaid didn't seem to hear. He looked from Benedict to Brazos with an unreadable expression on his face. "My daughters, gentlemen," he said. "All the family I have in the world. Two innocent young girls, living under a threat not of their making. Three weeks ago, Sarah was taking a meal out to some of my men riding the fence when a sniper's bullet struck the buckboard. She could have been killed. Perhaps the next time we shan't be so lucky … unless we can give them the protection they deserve …"

Hank Brazos swallowed painfully as he stared at the girls' fresh faces. In the simple lexicon of a one-time Texas cowboy, women were next to sacred, whether they be hardened saloon chippies, octogenarian grand-mothers, or daughters of rich ranchers like this. Brazos prided himself on the fact that never had he been unkind to a member of the fair sex, and not once had he turned a deaf ear to the plea of a woman in distress. The thought that these two girls might be living in fear of their lives caused a hard, tight lump to settle in the pit of his belly. Then, looking at Benedict, he wasn't surprised to see that the Yank seemed about as uncomfortable as he felt.

Benedict shifted his weight uneasily from one foot to the other. He had the suspicious feeling that Burk Kincaid had deliberately brought his daughters here to use as a weapon in his argument. He resented the cattleman's tactics, but the resentment was lost every time he looked at Emma Kincaid.

She was, without doubt, as pretty as a heart flush. And there were

15

few men whose admiration for attractive women was as honest and enthusiastic as Duke Benedict's. He had often reflected, sometimes happily, often regretfully, that woman was his Achilles' heel, and at that moment he felt his heel itch again.

He cleared his throat, then he eyed Brazos. The massive Texan shrugged. Duke Benedict dropped his cigar and ground it under his heel, his dark brows knit together in a frown. Could it be different this time? he asked himself. Might it be possible to hire their guns and prove a mere deterrent to the enemy? It happened like that sometimes. He was weakening.

And Kincaid sensed it. "We really do need you and Brazos, Mr. Benedict. I and my daughters … we need you desperately."

Benedict drew in a deep breath. Then Emma Kincaid said: "Father, I don't think we have the right to ask these gentlemen to involve themselves in our affairs."

"Nor do I," plain Sarah put in. "It doesn't seem fair."

That did it.

"Call the jailer if you will, Mr. Kincaid," Benedict said quietly. "Brazos, get your hat."

"Yes, sir." Hank Brazos grinned happily. He had known all along that the Yank would do the right thing in the end.

He always did when the chips were down.

2

The Big Land

CURLY CALEM said, "What's that fool bull takin' on about?" Leaning against the meat house wall, ramrod Stacey Blaine looked across the low knoll towards the pen that housed the Anvil's prize bull, Curway Masters Vivian the Fourth. "He doesn't need no reason to get his tail in a crack," he answered. "He starts cuttin' up if a quail sets on his fence."

"Yeah," murmured Calem. He was the Anvil's horse-breaker, a medium-sized man with a trim, muscular physique and an open, sun-brown face. He turned back to the repair job they were doing on the broken horse collar, but the bull's bellow shook the air again. Curly Calem swore and straightened. "We'd best take a look, Stacey. The galoot might've got his big head stuck between the rails again."

The gangling ramrod nodded and the two started for the knoll.

It was late afternoon on the Anvil Ranch and the whole land seemed to glow and blossom in the clear light. There was new grass underfoot and spring sunlight dappled the backs of the sleek red cattle strung out along the gentle slope of a hill. Crickets and cicadas vied for supremacy with the lowing of cows, and the bull frequently drowned out all other sounds with his indignant bellowing.

The big buildings of the Anvil stood on flat ground with undulating rangeland stretching away on all sides. The main homestead, which Burk Kincaid shared with his two daughters, faced east, with a five-acre fruit orchard directly behind it. The second house, which the cattleman had

17

built for his son years ago, stood close by, a smaller but more graceful structure than the homestead. Then there were a group of other buildings—bunkhouses, barns, stables, harness shacks, corn sheds, a cookhouse—and a special corral and stall for Curway Masters Vivian the Fourth.

As the hands brought the fine new corral into sight, the bull let go with another tremendous roar.

It was the sound of a true aristocrat, and Burk Kincaid's two thousand dollar stud bull was nothing if not that. Curway Masters Vivian the Fourth, known disrespectfully amongst the lowly hands who lacked his fine breeding as "Stinker", was class from the tip of his healthy muzzle to the tip of his well-bred tail. His lineage dated back two centuries and there wasn't a single flaw to be found in his splendid pedigree. Champions all were the critter's descendants, generation after generation of aloof cows and feisty bulls, and Stinker was considered the ultimate, perfect outcome of the line.

Vivian was royalty, and as befitted royalty, boasted his own private domain, near enough to the house so that a close watch could be kept on him, but far enough away so his delicate temperament might not be adversely affected by all the noise and bustle. It had caused not a little resentment among the underpaid hands when they discovered how much Kincaid had paid for the stud bull, and some of them believed the bull had better accommodation than the men. There was some substance to this, for Kincaid certainly spared no expense in seeing that the bull was comfortably housed. The corral was big and built from beautiful redwood logs, and there was a spacious straw-lined shelter where Vivian could escape the elements or recover his energies at the end of a hard session of studding. One hand had the job of changing the straw every day. The man insisted he hated Vivian worse than his wife, and his wife had shot him in the foot twenty years ago before running off to California with a cough syrup salesman.

Just about everybody on the spread detested the bull both for his arrogance and the attention Kincaid lavished on him. But even his most vehement detractors couldn't deny that Stinker was a marvelous worker. It was Vivian's task to improve the bloodlines of the Anvil herds and he went about his work with an enthusiasm and efficiency that bordered on the awesome. After only one season, more than fifty calves were trotting around with Vivian's proud features, and before this season was out there would be at least that many more on the way.

"That critter just doesn't know how to quit," cook Boots Jenner had remarked once after watching the bull go about his duties. Ramrod Stacey Blaine had the sneaking feeling that it was more envy of Stinker's prowess in this department rather than his aloof ways that rubbed some of the men the wrong way.

Curly Calem grunted in disgust when they reached the corral to see the bull all alone in the middle of his yard, pawing up dust with not even a quail in sight.

"Look at that, will you, Stacey? He just wanted to bring us runnin', that's all. Ain't a blamed thing wrong with him."

The ramrod glanced around the corral. Seeing no sign of anything that might be responsible for the bull's mood, he turned away.

"Better get back to it then, Curly."

"Hell, let's stay and have a smoke first, Stacey. The job'll still be there when we get back."

The ramrod hesitated, then nodded in agreement. Stacey Blaine was a conscientious ramrod, but it was true they had been hard at it all day.

With cigarettes burning, the hands leaned against the corral fence and watched the bull who was still acting up. Sweat ran down their faces and hoof-stirred dust drifted overhead.

"Looked in on Sam at the house this mornin'," Calem grunted after a silence.

"How is he?" the ramrod asked. Cowboy Sam Macey had been shot up in a clash with Fifty-four ranchmen a week earlier.

"Comin'. Be another week or two afore he can work, though." Calem rested his back against the fence and looked at the taller man questioningly. "What do you make of these new guns the boss brought out last night, Stacey?"

Stacey Blaine was a deliberate, slow-talking man who always considered questions carefully before voicing an opinion. Finally he said, "They seem all right to me, Curly. Mebbe Benedict is a mite flashy for my taste, but the Texan seems like a straight-shooter." He frowned down at his cigarette. "The girls seem to like 'em well enough."

"You noticed that, too, huh?"

The ramrod nodded and both fell silent. Curly Calem often sat on the ranch house porch at night with pretty Emma Kincaid, and on the rare occasions when Sarah went to town for a function, Stacey Blaine invariably accompanied her. Though their relationship with the sisters was casual and strictly honorable, the hands considered themselves close to the girls and they didn't much take to the way Emma and Sarah had been fussing over the newcomers.

After a while, Blaine said in his slow way, "Don't know as how it's such a bright idea bringin' in two fellers like that, Curly. I know they're supposed to be just ridin' the spread to help keep things quiet, but I'm figurin' they won't act so quiet if somethin' busts out with the Fifty-four."

Calem's young face hardened. "Don't see as how the boss had much choice, Stacey. I've heard about them Brand brothers that Tucker's put on. Folks say they're poison."

Blaine watched the bull. Vivian had stopped bellowing and was now moving warily towards his shelter.

"It's foolish, Curly," Blaine said. "The whole damned feud. There's room enough for the boss and Tucker out here. Why don't they just forget their feelin's and live peaceable?"

"I don't know what started things off in the first place, Stacey." Calem looked at the ramrod probingly. "You know what's between the boss and Tucker, don't you, Stacey?"

"Some of it," Blaine said. He'd been on the Anvil longer than any hand. He had worked on the spread back in the days when Kincaid's wild son had been here. Men like Calem often tried to find out why Virgil Kincaid had quit the Anvil, for the mystery surrounding his disappearance after a clash with his father seemed in some way associated with Kincaid's bitter feud with Joe Tucker. But today, as always, the ramrod refused to be drawn out on the matter.

"That's all in the past and ought to stay there, Curly," he said with an air of finality. "But I still say them two new hands are liable to stir things up unless Mr. Kincaid makes it plain to them that—"

The ramrod broke off with a startled exclamation that caused Calem to whirl and face the corral. A black-and-white streak of a dog had exploded from the bull's shelter to make a high-speed charge at the bull's black muzzle. Vivian roared and tossed his mighty horns. The barrel-chested dog came around from behind. Teeth nipped expensive heels and the hound flashed off and ducked beneath the lower rails before the bull could reach him with his horns.

The dog had moved so fast that it wasn't until he had emerged from the dust that the hands realized it was Brazos' battle-scarred trail hound, Bullpup.

"Well, I'll be damned!" Calem panted, reaching for a stone. "That's what was irkin' him." He threw the stone. "Go on, get to hell, you flea-bitten son of a bitch!"

His aim was good. The stone bounced off Bullpup's iron-ribbed flank. Calem didn't know the risk he took. Brazos' dog was prone to respond to that sort of treatment with his teeth. But Calem was lucky that Bullpup was preoccupied with the two thousand dollars' worth of pedigree on the hoof through the fence, and now he bounded forward to bark and infuriate Vivian just that much the more.

It was purely the bull's superior air, which was as noticeable to a mere dog as it was to a human, that had aroused Bullpup's interest in the first place. Wandering around headquarters while his master and Benedict were out familiarizing themselves with the ranch, Bullpup had ultimately found his way to the handsome corral, where he'd been almost deafened by Vivian's challenging voice.

Bullpup had been prepared to let the bull go on roaring and pawing if that was what he liked to do. But when he realized just how big and blown up with his own importance the creature was, he had decided that Curway Masters Vivian could do with a little trimming down.

The result had been a running battle over the past half hour with honors definitely going to the dog, Bullpup was an old hand with cattle and knew just how to get in quick, strike, then hightail it before the counter-attack could be mounted.

He decided it was time for one more pass, and he nipped in under the rail. Calem swore again, snatched up another stone and let it fly. The rock missed its mark, but bounced close enough to distract the dog for a vital moment. Then a sweeping horn found him. The horn didn't go in, but curved under the dog's belly, then threw him high. Bullpup yelped going up and snarled coming down. Dropping belly-flat under the bull's follow-up charge, he went in under the head and struck for the throat.

Calem and Blaine were both piling over the fence when a piercing whistle sounded from atop the knoll, followed by a booming voice:

"Hey, you old camp-robber! Get outa there and have some sense!"

At the sound of Brazos' voice, Bullpup immediately released his grip on the bull. He ducked under the corral rails, then trotted off to greet the approaching horsemen, wagging his tail proudly. Suddenly he propped and turned to watch the commotion as two fast-moving Anvil hands got over the fence just ahead of the raging bull who slammed his big head hard into a rail bare inches from Stacey Blaine's long legs.

"Sorry about that, gents," Brazos grinned as he rode up with Benedict. "I've tried to teach the varmint good manners, but he's just got a maverick streak in him, I guess." He reined in and leaned his big hands on the saddle pommel. "No damage, is there?"

Blaine was panting heavily. Calem, who'd tripped as he landed on the safe side of the fence, now scowled up at Brazos, his face covered in dust. The cowboy started to swear, but Blaine talked over him:

"No real damage done, Hank. Might be an idea to keep your dog away from the bull, though. The boss-man wouldn't take it kindly if he was to get tore up any."

"Reckon he wouldn't at that," Brazos said with an appraising glance at the bull. Then he shook a finger at the dog. "No more bull-baitin'," he said emphatically. "Compre? No more bull!"

"That would be a change—for both of you," Benedict drawled. Then he turned to the hands. "Any developments while we were away?"

Blaine shook his head. "How'd you make out?"

"Well, we rode the full length of the border between Anvil and the Fifty-four," Benedict said. "We checked with the hands and everything was quiet."

Brazos started to speak but was drowned out by the bull. He motioned to the others and they moved off over the hill, then started down the slope to headquarters together.

"We sighted three fellers on the Fifty-four side out by Three Buttes, Stacey," he said when he could make himself heard. "They seemed to be watchin' the North Forty. That anythin' new?"

Blaine shook his head. "Not really. They keep a watch on us and we keep a watch on them." His jaw went hard. "That's the way things are hereabouts these days. Watchin' and waitin', waitin' and watchin'. Then some fool gets trigger-happy and you've got buryin' to do afore you go back to watchin' and waitin'.'"

Brazos stepped down when they reached the yard. "You don't think much of this fracas, I take it, Stacey?"

Blaine rested bony hands on his hips and looked sober. "That I don't," he confessed. His brows lifted fractionally. "It'd probably bother me more than it would fellers like you though, I'd reckon."

Brazos frowned. "Don't know what you mean."

"I think I do," Benedict said, dismounting. He looped the reins over his arm and inclined his head at the ramrod. "I get the impression that you believe we're the sort of men who might thrive on violence and disorder. Would that be so, Mr. Blaine?"

"Could be," the ramrod answered.

"Then you're wrong," Benedict said. "The reason we're here—the sole reason—is to maintain the peace and to afford the Kincaids the protection that …" he paused deliberately and looked from one man to the other before concluding, "… that Anvil hands seem unwilling or unable to give."

"Judas, what'd you have to go and say a thing like that for, Benedict?" Brazos growled after a red-faced Calem and a tight-lipped Blaine suddenly spun on their heels and strode away. "Wasn't any call for that, as I see it."

"I believe there was," Benedict replied sharply. "Whether you were aware of it or not, that ramrod implied that we're nothing better than hired guns. I resent that implication.. I resent it very much."

"Is *that* what he was sayin'?" Brazos said with a furrowed brow. He looked indignant. "Well, by Judas, I resent it, too. I oughta give him a piece of my—"

"Catch him the next time around, Texan," Benedict said with a smile, his testiness vanishing as quickly as it had come. "Come on, let's turn the horses in, wash up and get on to the house. We're invited for supper with the Kincaids, remember? I'm hungry enough to eat chips."

Lights showed from the house windows by the time they left the wash-house and started up the slope. The air was filled with the sweet evening smells of sage and flower blossoms. There was a picture postcard quality about the scene with the big house standing against the dark of the orchard and the dying light in the sky beyond.

"Sure looks peaceful, don't it, Yank?" Brazos drawled.

"That it does. And it's our job to keep it that way."

Bullpup took a playful nip at Brazos' heels. The Texan kicked him and the dog rolled, then came into the attack again, growling with mock ferocity. Brazos laughed, jumped over the hound, almost stumbled, then looked up to see Benedict staring at him coldly.

"Eighty a month," Benedict said tersely. "Surely they could have hired a court jester for less than that."

Brazos just grinned and clapped a hand on Benedict's shoulder. "Sometimes you take things too serious, Yank. You get to frettin' about what might happen, when ofttimes it never does."

Though reluctant to accept advice from Hank Brazos on anything outside the fundamentals of trailsmanship and such, Benedict realized the Texan was probably right. There was no need for trouble to erupt here on the Anvil, he told himself, providing they worked hard at keeping it at bay.

And the situation didn't seem as dangerous as he had at first suspected, he was forced to admit. Of course, there was tension between the spreads, but he had the impression that the Anvil riders were little interested in fighting. If the Fifty-four men could be convinced that violence would prove costly, it was possible that the whole ugly business would end.

He felt positive of this as they entered the house, but his improving mood was quickly put to the test. Sarah and Emma waited for them in the study. So far so good. Emma had poured drinks, and that was even better. But then, as Benedict put on his best smile for Emma's benefit and prepared to launch into the light chatter at which he was such an expert, pretty Emma drew Brazos down to the chaise longue beside her and insisted he tell her how he had found his first full day on Anvil.

Brazos blushed, as he always did in the close company of a pretty girl, then he started to talk.

Benedict stared incredulously. Hank Brazos, though a tolerably engaging man at times, was an illiterate country boy who wore purple shirts.

Duke Benedict, by contrast, was a gentleman of refinement and perception with a Harvard education to boot. Surely Emma Kincaid could tell where the real quality lay?

Then he comforted himself with a thought. She was a sweet and considerate young lady. She saw that Brazos was a fumble-footed rube and was merely doing what any good hostess would do to put her guest at ease. So, certain that he was right, he didn't mind turning to Sarah and giving her the benefit of his witty dialogue while he waited for Emma to get through with Brazos. But another unpleasant surprise greeted him. After a few minutes, Sarah Kincaid pointed out that she was wearing a new dress. Did he like it? She hoped he did.

Benedict's jaw sagged. The plain-faced girl had taken a shine to him. This couldn't be permitted to go any farther, he told himself firmly. There was an unwritten law in this two-man partnership—Duke Benedict walked off with the pretty girls and Hank Brazos took the plain ones to church.

"Miss, Emma," he said with his most handsome smile, "did I tell you about the time I had dinner with the President of the United States?"

The girl looked up at him vaguely, then turned back to Brazos, "And did you see Blue Valley, Hank?" she smiled. "No? Well, I shall take you out there at the first opportunity. It's my favorite place on Anvil. I'm sure you'll love it."

"Shucks, I just bet I will if you like it, Miss Emma."

Benedict banged a hand against the side of his head. No. There was nothing wrong with his hearing, for he heard the dinner gong quite clearly.

Sarah slipped an arm through his and smiled. "This way, Duke."

Too stunned to protest, Benedict looked back over his shoulder as they left the room. Brazos had Emma on his arm and didn't seem to know how to stop grinning.

The heady odors of steak and chilis wafted out to them from the dining room. Thirty minutes ago Duke Benedict had felt hungry enough to eat chips. Suddenly he found himself without the vestige of an appetite.

Was it possible, he asked himself, that there had been some sad oversight in pretty Emma's upbringing that was responsible for her inability to recognize a knight on a snow-white charger when he showed up?

He smiled at himself. It must be true what they sometimes said, he reflected in a rare moment of self-appraisal: he was too damned vain and assured for his own good.

But of course the situation could not be permitted to continue, he told himself firmly, readily accepting this challenge to the Benedict charm. Brazos' rustic simplicity might have helped him win the first round, but the fight had only just begun.

3

Brothers of the Gun

STARS began to appear in the night sky as the three Fifty-four men sat down on the bunkhouse steps and took out their tobacco.

Hogger Smith was angry. Al Stock and Jim Chester could always tell when the big waddy was in one of his bad moods by the way he clamped his broad mouth shut and breathed noisily through his hairy black nostrils. Though curious to know the reason for Smith's annoyance, the cowhands didn't attempt to probe. Big Hogger had the longest reach and the shortest temper on the Fifty-four, and you could never be sure when his spleen would be directed at you personally. It was always better to wait until Hogger felt good and ready to speak of his own accord.

The wind that had risen with dusk clanked the old Halliday wind pump across the yard. Up at the house, Joe Tucker could just be seen seated in his huge old chair on the porch. From the house came the sounds of rattling pots and pans. Miss Cass would be washing up, the hands reflected. When she finished, she would come out and sit in her rocker and watch the night come down. They wouldn't talk much. Joe could talk with the best of them, but Miss Cass seldom had much to say.

Al Stock flicked ash from his cigarette with a finger, then looked up as Hogger Smith turned his head and spat.

"It ain't right," Hogger declared.

It was their cue. "What ain't, Hogger?" Chester asked.

The big cowboy glowered. "That the boss should post these gunnies above us, of course."

"Has he done that?" Stock asked, surprised.

Smith's head bobbed. "You goddamn know it! I was out to the sump this afternoon. That yeller-headed Flint Brand showed up on that flashy palomino of his'n. Told me to get across and check on the boys at Three Buttes. I told him to go fry. He told me I'd do like he said or he'd fix it so I got to walkin' crooked."

Two astonished cowhands gaped. Surely nobody would have the gall to talk to Hogger that way? Particularly somebody who had been on the Fifty-four for only two days!

But it was true. "I told him to go fry again," Smith went on bitterly. "You know what he done?" Two heads shook in unison and Hogger Smith's indignation mounted as he approached the cause and nugget of his wrath. "The little bastard put his hand on his gun."

Chester and Stock were suitably shocked.

"I thought the boss hired that pair to watch over us," Al Stock said thickly.

"That's what I thought," Smith said. "But I tell you somethin', boys, with gun sharks like that you just don't ever know what way they're gonna jump. They ain't like you and me, not that dirty breed. They figure gun speed gives 'em rights to do what they like to who they want. But take their Colts away and they ain't anythin' but gutless nothin's. And, if you ask me, that Flint Brand is the biggest gutless nothin' of all."

Ram Brand came out of the deepening gloom along the side of the cookhouse so swiftly and silently that he was in their midst before they realized it. The older and bigger of the gunfighter brothers stood there with his hands on his narrow hips and his brutal pale face twisted as he stared down at Smith. Chester and Stock edged away. Hogger Smith stared up defiantly.

"You've got a big mouth, Smith," Brand said.

"What I said ain't nothin' but the truth, Brand."

"Is that so? You were bad-namin' my brother—you who's nothin' better than a plaster-gutted, hollowed-out, tenth-rate son of a bitch."

"I've got a right to my say, Brand."

"And I've got a right to do *this.*"

Brand swung and hit Smith hard in the mouth. He then kicked him in the belly and the cowboy doubled up and screamed in agony. Brand cuffed him viciously to both sides of the head as he tumbled down the steps. Then he seized Smith's thatch and jerked his head down and slammed up with his knee. Smith fell and twitched.

Suddenly the night was filled with shouts and men came running from all directions. Ram Brand stepped back from the unconscious cowhand, his right hand wrapped around the butt of his gun. His brother came from the bunkhouse with the others, took one look at Smith and then whirled around.

"Did you do this, Ram?"

"He was puttin' his dirty mouth on you, Flint," Ram said. Then he jerked his head as Tucker came shouldering through the men. "He asked for it and he got it."

Joe Tucker knelt at Smith's side, touched his bloody face, then rose slowly.

"What happened?" he asked woodenly.

They told him and Joe Tucker swung savagely on Ram Brand. "You had no call to beat up on Smith that way, Brand. You might have maimed him for life."

Ram Brand's eyes flared, but he compressed his lips, waiting for his brother to speak. Though smaller and younger than Ram, Flint was the gunman with the bigger reputation and the quicker mind. Ram was the bludgeon of the deadly partnership, slim Flint the rapier.

"Seems to me Smith *was* askin' for it, Tucker," Flint said. "Can't hold it against a man for stickin' up for his brother, can you?"

"Stickin up for you is one thing, but smashin' a good hand up that way is another," Tucker retorted. He paused as a cowboy hurried up with a pail of water that he poured over Smith. The big man twitched, groaned and started to come to. Tucker was about to speak again when his daughter came through the circle of cowboys. Her thin face showing pale in the gloom, Cass Tucker looked down at Smith and then turned slowly to face the Brands.

"Why did you do this?" she asked. Her voice was quiet, but it carried such heavy reproof that Ram fidgeted and stared down at his boots. Even the narrow-faced Flint sounded almost apologetic when he spoke.

"Things like this just happen sometimes, Miss Cass. Ram never meant to maim Smith, just to quiet him down some."

Cass Tucker continued to stare at the gunmen in heavy silence. Nobody spoke. The cattleman's daughter was considered strange and cold by the men of the Fifty-four, but she was respected by all. There was a strength in Cass that extended far beyond the limitation of her frail body.

Finally she turned to her father and said, "You will have to let them go, Father. It was wrong to bring them here in the first place. They don't belong here."

"Later, Cass," Tucker said, breathing heavily. "We'll talk about it later."

"Things won't be any different later," she said flatly, then walked away, the men opening their ranks once more to let her pass.

"I want to speak to you men in private," Tucker said to the Brands, and they followed him across the yard towards the water trough. The rancher stopped by the trough and stared off in the direction of the hills that marked the boundary with the Anvil ranch.

"I hired you fellers because I felt I had to," Tucker said harshly, not looking at them. "I know you're hard men with hard ways. I reckon as how you've got to be or you wouldn't be any good in your line of work." He turned abruptly. "But I'm not havin' hired gun packers beat up my own men. If I wanted that, there are plenty of Anvil men who'll do it for nothin'." His eyes cut sharply at Ram. "You hear that good, mister?"

Ram Brand looked petulant. "I hear good enough, I reckon."

"Then don't you forget it. And you see that he doesn't, Flint."

"Whatever you say, boss-man."

Tucker rubbed his face, staring back at the bunkhouse. "Kickin' the stuffin' out of a man just because he—"

"Boss-man," Flint cut in softly, "you've made your point. You told us what you want and we said we'll do it. But don't carry on about it, Mr. Tucker. I get nervous when folks start carryin' on."

Joe Tucker stiffened. Flint Brand was a slim, dangerous silhouette in the starlight. A harsh retort came to the cattleman's lips but died there. He had to remind himself that he was dealing with a new and unfamiliar breed of man here. There was a lot he had to learn about gunslingers and their touchy ways.

"Don't like gettin' nervous," Flint murmured after a thick silence, then he touched Ram's elbow and led the way across the yard.

A big sigh came from Tucker as he turned and trudged towards the house. He stopped when he saw the slim silhouette by the wind pump stand. Cass didn't speak as she moved out to join him, but he knew she must have heard everything.

They walked up to the big old house that Joe Tucker had built back in the good days. Mounting the steps, the rancher went to his great chair on the porch, threw himself into it and reached for his bottle. Cass stood by an upright with the wind tossing her hair about her face.

"It's all wrong, Pa," she said. "All of it is wrong."

"Don't tell me, young lady," he said angrily. "Go tell that hate-loco man on the Anvil. Go tell him it's foolish to hire gunslingers when enough good men are dyin' without their help anyway. Go tell Burk Kincaid to get rid of them gun whelps he's hired, then mebbe I'll get rid of the Brands. Why don't you do that instead of chewin' at me all the time?"

"Are you certain Mr. Kincaid has hired gunfighters, Pa?"

"Of course I am. A Texan and a dude named Benedict. Stock spotted 'em riding the border this mornin'. He's got 'em right enough."

"Has it occurred to you that he mightn't have felt the need to hire men like that if you hadn't brought the Brands in?"

Tucker's eyes flashed in the darkness. "Has it damn well occurred to you that I wouldn't have needed the Brands if the Anvil riders hadn't shot Brick Dolan down at the creek last month?"

"Brick was one man, Pa. There will be lots more dead men if you keep those horrible killers on. You know that, don't you?"

"You're wearyin' me, Cass. Ain't I got enough worries?"

"I'm sorry, Pa." She moved to the doorway. "Want some coffee?"

"No, just a little peace."

Cass walked through the front room with its tattered Indian relics, then down the hall to the kitchen. In the cheerless but well-scrubbed room she paused by the lamp and looked down at her trembling hands. There were chores to be done before she retired, but suddenly they seemed unimportant after what had happened. She brushed a strand of hair back from her face and went through to her room, the only thing in Cass Tucker's world that she considered exclusively her own. It was her small, feminine haven away from the rough and gritty world of men. The room faced east to catch the morning sun. It was painted a soft green and contained a bed with a yellow counterpane, two chairs and a bureau. One wall was lined with books.

This room was the sanctuary to which Cass always retired whenever the harshness of her existence became too much for her. It was filled with mementoes of her lonely life, one of which she treasured above all: a beautifully framed daguerreotype that stood on the bureau with fresh flowers in a tiny glass vase beside it.

She moved slowly across to the bureau now, then sat on the edge of her bed and gazed at the picture, her face softening.

The daguerreotype showed a handsome boy with blue eyes and a reckless, laughing mouth. His hair was long and there was something about him that radiated vitality plus a wildness that nothing could tame.

The picture was of Virgil Kincaid, Burk Kincaid's only son.

***

Burk Kincaid looked pensive as he handed Benedict and Brazos their first week's wages. Seated behind his big desk in the study with afternoon sunlight glowing on the rich Brussels carpet behind him, the boss of the Anvil frowned as they pocketed the money, then he turned his swivel chair so he faced the window.

Benedict and Brazos exchanged glances. Though they had been riding the Anvil for a full week now, neither felt he had come to know Kincaid very well. The rancher was a solitary man, a little aloof, always dignified but never really friendly. His employees and his daughters seemed to hold the cattleman in awe. But awe didn't come easily to either Duke Benedict or Hank Brazos. After a long silence, Benedict spoke up boldly.

"Something troubling you, Mr. Kincaid?"

"No, not really, I suppose, Mr. Benedict," the rancher replied.

"You don't sound too sure," Brazos put in. The Texan stood with his weight on one leg, a hip out-thrust, dominating the room with his bulk.

Kincaid turned and regarded them speculatively. Then he picked up a pen and started tapping it against the desk top. "I suppose that what concerns me," he said finally, "is the feeling that everything is going too well."

"Is that a problem?" Benedict smiled.

There was no answering smile from the rancher. "The problem, Mr. Benedict," he said thinly, "is that a rattler going to ground is not necessarily any the less dangerous. Sometimes it simply means that he's waiting a more fortuitous time to attack."

"Well, it ain't been all *that* quiet," said Brazos.

This was true. There had been several minor incidents along the Anvil-Fifty-four border during the past week, but the presence of Brazos and Benedict, plus a little luck, had seen these sputter out without developing into anything serious. With the roundup in full swing on both ranches and no fenced border between them, men and cattle often strayed close to the borders at times. Shots had been fired on three such occasions, once from the Anvil and twice from the Fifty-four, but they had merely been warnings.

"I still don't like it," Kincaid said. "I have the uneasy feeling that the Fifty-four is planning something." He looked up at Benedict. "You don't agree?"

"No, I don't," Benedict replied. "Do you want to know what I think of the situation, Mr. Kincaid?"

"Yes."

"Have you ever heard the term, Mexican stand-off?"

"Yes."

"Well, that's what we have here. Border fights between cattle outfits are nothing new, Mr. Kincaid, for cowhands are all too often a quarrelsome breed. But gunfighters are something else again. They introduce a serious element into what may have been regarded before as something not much more serious than a little horseplay. I'm not saying that the struggle between the Anvil and the Fifty-four was that harmless, far from it, but I feel quite certain that Tucker's hiring of the Brands, followed by your signing us on, has had the effect of calming the hands down. Nobody really wants to die, Mr. Kincaid, and death is always close when gunslingers buy into a game." He shrugged. "I believe that's how things stand at the moment."

Kincaid glanced at Brazos. "Do you agree with Mr. Benedict?"

"I do on this."

"Hmm." Kincaid dipped his pen in the inkwell and started to write. "Very well, that will be all, gentlemen."

Two thoughtful men made their way from the study, walked down the hallway and emerged on the long front gallery. There they halted. Brazos rubbed the back of his neck and Benedict stared back down the hallway. Both were frowning.

"You feelin' an itch where you can't get at it to scratch, Yank?" Brazos said.

"I wouldn't phrase it exactly that way," Benedict said, "but it assesses my feelings accurately enough."

"I figured Kincaid would be right pleased with the way things are goin'. I mean, I don't want to blow my own bugle, but I reckon we've been makin' a tolerable good fist of this here job of work."

"We are; an excellent job."

"Then what's chewin' his liver?"

Benedict moved to the balcony railing and stared out over the rolling acres of the Anvil spread. "It's possible that Kincaid really does believe this may be just a lull before the storm."

Brazos rubbed his neck some more, looked at Benedict obliquely, then slouched across to stand on the top step. "I've got a thick idea in my head that just don't make sense no how, Yank—"

"Another one?" Benedict said caustically. Then he smiled. "Let me hear it."

Brazos was very sober as he turned his shaggy head. "I had a hunch in there just now that Kincaid was actin' kind of disappointed 'cause things ain't been livelier. Crazy, huh?"

"Crazy, even by your standards," Benedict snapped back. "Preposterous."

"Guess so."

"The man is simply nervous. Sometimes peace can be as harrowing as war itself—if one is expecting the war to break out all the time. It's up to us to convince Kincaid that the peace can be permanent."

Brazos thought this sounded like good sense. It was imperative that they keep the peace. And they were able to do just that for another full week—until that late afternoon when the peace was broken out at Three Buttes. Violently.

4

Slaughter at Three Buttes

THE whole thing had been an accident, and Curly Calem couldn't understand why the Fifty-four men didn't realize this as he lay pinned down with two other punchers as Fifty-four men fired down at them from a ridge above.

It had started while new men Hanlon and Feller were driving a sizeable group of cattle across the North Forty for the branding yards at the Five Mile. Something spooked the cows as they approached Three Buttes and they stampeded towards the Fifty-four ranch. On their way out from the branding camp to help bring the cattle in, Calem and Jim Crocker saw Feller and Hanlon riding in hot pursuit clear across the border. They fired off their guns and yelled to the hands to come back, but they hadn't been heard and Calem and Crocker had no option but to give chase in the hope of catching the hands before Fifty-four scouts did.

As it panned out, they caught up with Hanlon and Feller at the same moment a group of Fifty-four riders appeared atop the high red ridge that sloped up to Three Buttes. Immediately the Fifty-four horsemen had opened up, and the Anvil men, caught in the open, had had no option but to take cover among the boulders at the ridge base.

Calem cursed now as a fresh hail of lead came down and he was forced to worm his way deep beneath the shallow cutback that protected him. Runty Hud Feller lay a short distance away, sprawled in the slough grass beside his horse. Feller had been hit in the first volley, killed on his third day on the ranch. Calem had a shoulder crease, but it didn't hurt much. Hanlon and Crocker were still all right as far as Calem knew.

"Curly!" It was Zeke Hanlon's voice.

"Yeah?"

"They're movin' down!"

Cautiously, Calem lifted his head and peered up. For a moment he could see nothing but the towering ramparts of the buttes, and the shimmer of sun on talus and grass. But then he saw a man leap up, scurry a short distance down the steep ridge slope and dive behind a small boulder.

Calem ducked his head, then rolled swiftly towards the boulders. Enemy guns churned, but the fire was wild and he made it safely to Hanlon's position.

"They ain't gonna wait until dark like I figured, Zeke," Calem panted. "How you holdin' out for slugs?"

"Gettin' low." The hand's voice shook. He was only a kid.

Kincaid had signed Hanlon and Feller up just to help with the roundup.

"Don't lose your grip, kid," Calem said firmly. "We ain't dead and done for yet."

"As good as dead, I reckon, Curly," panted lean Jim Crocker, crawling into sight through the rocks, dragging a bloody leg. "I just got a sight of them blond-headed gun packers comin' down with the others."

"The Brands!" Curly Calem paled. The tough horse wrangler was no coward, but he was no gunfighter either. With the Fifty-four men outnumbering them two-to-one, and with the Brands among them, their chances of getting out of this were extremely slim. Then he grew aware of Crocker and Hanlon looking at him and he put on his toughest grin. "We got the advantage here, boys," he said with forced confidence. "We're in here and they've got to root us out. Just lay low, hold your fire, and when you get a target make certain you don't miss."

"I just don't understand it, Curly," young Hanlon said, close to tears. "We did nothing but chase them cows. And poor Hud, he—"

"Stiffen up, Hanlon!" Calem rapped. "Check that gun out and make sure it's loaded. Keep sharp!"

With trembling hands, Hanlon broke open the gun. Calem looked at Crocker who was sweating so hard he could barely see. Curly Calem felt his guts tighten as he heard the sounds of men drawing closer. So this was how it was going to be. He'd always figured to die in bed, preferably with Emma as his gray-headed wife bending over him. But if this was how it was to be, then he was damned if he would let any Fifty-four polecat see him scared. He popped up, snapped a shot at a twisting, running figure, and grunted in satisfaction as the man screamed out and fell.

His shot brought a storm of lead in return. Bullets peppered the boulders and howled off in screaming ricochets. Crocker and Hanlon huddled close to him, their eyes desperately pleading for the help he couldn't give. He waited through a timeless moment of apprehension, then he slowly grew aware that other guns were blasting from higher up.

Puzzled, Calem lifted his head. Suddenly a running man appeared close by. Calem jerked up his gun but didn't fire. The Fifty-four man ran with jerky steps, eyes stretched wide, a growing stain of crimson on his shirt.

He was a running dead man.

They heard the man crash down, then Crocker found the nerve to bob his head up and take a look. He almost fell back down, his eyes stretched wide in amazement.

"It's Brazos and Benedict, Curly!" he gasped. "They're up on the ridge!"

As an astounded Curly Calem lifted his head, a cry of pain sounded from close by. The Anvil man had a glimpse of the towering Ram Brand staggering away favoring his left leg. Lead howled down from above and Brazos' booming voice sounded above the guns.

"Ride out, Fifty-four, or we'll bury the bunch of you!"

Brazos wasn't boasting. Caught short of the security of the rocks where the Anvil trio were hidden, and with sparse cover behind, the Fifty-four men were in no-man's-land. Flint Brand shouted an order and the attackers broke and ran, sprinting towards the hill country to the west. Lead peppered the ground behind the fleeing figures, and a wide-eyed Curly Calem realized that the twin guns above were no longer shooting to kill.

Mouthing a curse, Calem jumped up and opened fire on the running men. The next instant a bullet hit rock a bare foot from his head. He turned to see Benedict and Brazos sliding their mounts down the ridge slope towards them.

37

"Let them go, Calem!" Benedict shouted.

"Let 'em go?" Crocker gasped. "What the hell kind of gun-packers are they anyways, Curly?"

Calem wasn't sure. All he knew was that a gunfighter who showed compassion with the enemy at his mercy was a new breed to him.

Brazos checked his horse near the boulders while Benedict rode down to where two Fifty-four men had fallen.

"Who's that lyin' out there by the horse?" Brazos panted. "Is it Feller?"

"Yeah. He stopped one early, Hank," Calem said. "Hell, man, where did you come from? We were done for, for sure."

"We heard the shootin' as we come up by the Five Mile," Brazos supplied, stepping down. Then he called, "What have you got there, Yank?"

"One dead, one wounded!" was Benedict's response from the rocks.

"Wounded?" Jim Crocker said, cocking his gun. "I'll soon fix that."

As Crocker rounded a boulder he saw Al Stock of the Fifty-four sprawled panting and bloodied in the slough grass. Benedict stood beside the man with his six-gun trained on Crocker's chest.

Crocker stopped as if he'd run into an invisible wall. Benedict cocked his hammer back and the Anvil man jumped backwards.

"Hell, Duke, what you pointin' that at me for?" Crocker yelped.

A big hand pushed Crocker from behind, sending him stumbling forward.

"You don't shoot wounded men, Crocker," Hank Brazos growled. "Even in the war we never did that."

Crocker looked in bewilderment from Hanlon and Calem to Brazos and Benedict. "But ... but two minutes ago he was tryin' to kill us!"

"Two men dead, Crocker," Benedict said bitterly as he lowered his six-gun. "Isn't that enough for you?"

Crocker looked helplessly at Curly Calem. But he found no help there, for Calem's confounded expression matched his own.

"They ... they attacked us without warnin', Duke," Calem said uncertainly. "You'd show a man mercy who did that?"

"We had no choice, Crocker," Al Stock grimaced from the grass. "The Brands said we had to hit you, so we hit. Better to tangle with you than with them."

Brazos looked across at Benedict. From the moment they had sighted the Brands from the ridge above, they had guessed how it had been. It took a special breed of man to trigger an attack like this, and somehow they didn't believe the Fifty-four hands measured up to it.

Benedict's handsome face showed pale in the dying light as he housed his gun. "Get the horses and load up the dead," he said, tight-jawed.

"What about Stock?" Calem asked.

"We'll send him to the doctor in town."

"The boss ain't gonna take kindly to that," Crocker said hesitantly.

"Won't take kindly to common decency?" Benedict rapped out. "He'll take it, mister, and he'll take it kindly. So will you. Now get busy!"

Curly Calem shook his head in wonder. This definitely was not a breed he had struck before. He trudged off slowly to help round up the horses. It was sundown and cool now, and for the first time he realized just how much his shoulder hurt.

***

The deadly clash between the Anvil and Fifty-four ranches at Three Buttes set a spark to the tinderbox in Keogh County that threatened to explode into a full-blooded conflagration.

The day after they buried Hud Feller, a party of Anvil riders, acting on their own initiative, hit the southern plains of the Fifty-four, stampeding a herd of stock and wounding Jim Chester in a brief clash.

The Fifty-four hit back at dawn the next day, launching an attack of the Five Mile muster site, leaving seventeen dead or wounded beeves behind them before Flint Brand led them back across the border into Fifty-four territory.

It was learned later that Flint Brand had planned and led the attack to square accounts for Ram, who was still out of action from his wound taken at Three Buttes.

The three days that followed reminded Benedict and Brazos of isolated skirmishes during the Civil War. Only this was peace-time Nevada, not war-time Tennessee or Virginia.

During that week, the Anvil's trouble-shooters earned their high fees many times over. In their saddles day and night, singly or together, they rode the wide stretches of the Anvil spread, often the target of snipers' rifles. But at all times theirs were the voices of moderation on the Anvil, keeping the series of skirmishes from developing into full, all-out war.

The Three Buttes' fight firmly established the new men as the heroes of Anvil. Though Benedict worked the fastest guns and was obviously the brains of the partnership, Hank Brazos' popularity quickly exceeded Benedict's. Brazos, with his free-and-easy ways, his ranching background and his immense physical strength, was a man the cowboys could easily identify with. On the other hand, Benedict, with his clipped Eastern accent and natural arrogance, was a more aloof figure and they found it hard to understand and like him. However, there wasn't a man on the Anvil who didn't realize that, without high-stepping Duke Benedict, the situation would have been infinitely more dangerous. Benedict's presence alone proved a continual deterrent to the men of the Fifty-four.

That spring week proved to be almost as tense a time for the town of Sheridan as it was for the cattle outfits. In the past, the town had been an unofficial peace area to both factions, even though no hand from either ranch would dare walk its streets unarmed. But too many men were being shot in the struggle, and the enmities and resentments washed over into Sheridan. There were fistfights in the streets and two outbreaks of gunplay. Though Sheriff Rudkin and Deputy Eli Peachman struggled hard to keep control, it was feared that at any time somebody would get killed in Sheridan, and fear walked its streets like a tangible thing.

During that spring week two men had been killed, seven wounded, and scores of steers had been killed or rustled by both sides. It was a week that brought Joe Tucker and Burk Kincaid closer to the showdown that would resolve their hatred for each other that few people really understood.

And at the end of the week, General Montgomery H. Madison came to Sheridan.

***

Though standing less than five feet seven in his high-heeled cavalry boots, General Montgomery H. Madison was definitely larger than life.

It was six months since the commander of distant Fort Hook had been seen in Sheridan. "Flash" Madison they called him down south, and he certainly fitted the name. He wore his curly yellow hair past the collar of his gaudy buckskin jacket. His blond goatee was neatly trimmed, and his drooping moustache hid his little woman's mouth. But he was tough. And that day he assembled the protagonists of the Anvil-Fifty-four range war in the Sheridan Council Chambers, it was immediately plain that General Madison was hell-bent on reminding every man present just how tough he was.

"It will cease!" he thundered, slamming a small gloved fist down on the highly polished table top. "By heaven, I will see it cease or know the reason why!"

The combatants were lined up on either side of the long table under Madison's gimlet eye. Joe Tucker sat glumly in his chair with the Brand brothers flanking him.

Across from Tucker was Burt Kincaid, dignified and grim in an expensive linen suit. Looking even more immaculate than the rancher, in his best broadcloth suit and bed-of-flowers vest, Duke Benedict smoked a long black cigar and eyed the Brands expressionlessly.

Overwhelming his straight-backed chair at Benedict's side was Hank Brazos. As a former sergeant in the Confederate Army, the Texan was a little in awe of this sawn off little man who had been one of that army's most flamboyant and successful generals.

Stacey Blaine sat next to Brazos, with Sheriff Barney Rudkin at the end of the table. The sheriff, who was more intimidated by Madison than by his own skinny but volatile wife, jumped when Madison again banged the table and yelled. "Cease!"

Duke Benedict didn't jump. Carefully ashing his cigar, he looked at the little man and said quietly, "Wishing won't make it so, General. It will take more than saying 'cease' to bring this sorry business to a conclusion."

For a moment Madison's mouth hung open, then he scowled darkly and locked his hands behind his back. "Mr. Benedict," he said. "Former Union officer. Correct?"

"That's so."

"It couldn't be, Mr. Benedict, that you have brought some legacy of North-South enmity here to this conference table, could it?"

Benedict's eyes flashed. "I'm merely stating the situation as I see it, General. I was happy to come here today, and I'll be happier still if we walk out of here after reaching an amicable agreement."

Madison grunted, slightly mollified. "And what about everybody else? Are Mr. Benedict's sentiments generally shared? Mr. Tucker?"

"I'm here, ain't I, General?" Tucker said. "Wouldn't be here if I thought it was a waste of time."

"Well said, Mr. Tucker, well said. Mr. Kincaid?"

Burt Kincaid flicked a glance across at Tucker before he turned his gaze to the general. "I'm a peaceable man, General. Everybody knows that. But I must say here and now that I resent your sending out troopers to bring us in."

"Would you have attended this meeting otherwise?"

"I don't appreciate intimidation," Kincaid hedged.

"You would perhaps prefer the perpetuation of the reckless violence that has been turning this county into a shooting gallery, Mr. Kincaid?"

Kincaid sat up very straight. "I'm a busy man, General. I suggest that you get on with what you have to say and leave the innuendoes and sarcasm for another time."

"I guess that makes it pretty plain how *he* feels about makin' peace," Flint Brand said.

"Don't recall anybody askin' for your opinion, pilgrim," Brazos growled.

"Enough, enough!" Madison snapped. "Very well, Mr. Kincaid, acting upon your suggestion I shall attempt to do away with the preliminaries and lay my cards on the table."

Madison grew thoughtful as he moved away from his chair, hands clasped behind his back. He paused at the window to look out at the lawn where several of his blue-garbed troopers sat in the shade of a cottonwood. Then he turned.

"For the benefit of those who may be unaware of my position in this county, I have power that transcends that of all law enforcement agencies. My main concern has long been the Indian renegades along the borders, and I might remind you that those red devils take up my time most fully. But they are heathen savages who know no better, and one expects them to act in a warlike way." He paused, then added heavily: "But one does not expect the same from supposedly civilized white men."

He gave a little time for that to sink in, then came slowly back to the table.

"I have attempted, in the past, to get to the root of this enmity between Mr. Tucker and Mr. Kincaid, but with little success. I find this regrettable, but as further investigation into this matter would doubtless bring me up against the same old brick wall, I shan't waste time pursuing it here today."

He looked sharply at Kincaid and Tucker before continuing:

"The situation is intolerable. This is a free and supposedly lawful community, yet we have men dying and being shot up almost daily. Death has a loud voice, gentlemen, and what has been happening here in Keogh County has already reached Washington. And Washington wants to know what I intend doing about it. I shall furnish you with the answer I gave."

Here he paused again to send his blue-eyed gaze at the Brands, then at Benedict and Brazos.

"There are aspects of the law in this territory concerning such matters which unfortunately protect those primarily responsible. A man can hire another to pull a trigger for him, but past and costly experience in the law courts has established that the hirers are rarely convicted of a capital offence in such matters, guilty as they might be. However, the same does not apply to those who actively participate in the violence. And if any man present has any doubts, I refer to your two gunfighters. Mr. Tucker, and to yours, Mr. Kincaid."

Ram Brand sneered, "Can't land the big fish, so you go for the minnows, huh?"

"Silence, sir!" Madison snapped. "I do not write the laws—I merely see they are upheld, and by glory, I shall do that here! Do I make myself plain? If the excesses of this region do not cease forthwith, I shall return in force and rope you four in. Then, by heaven, I shall see to it that you are hit with the full force of law. Now, does anybody have a comment to make on that?" He glowered at Ram. "Constructive comment is what I am inviting."

"Sounds reasonable enough to me," Brazos grunted. "How about you, Yank?"

"Reasonable enough, I suppose," Benedict drawled. "Though it's probably unworkable."

"How do you mean?" Madison asked.

Benedict eyed him steadily. "My partner and I signed on with

43

Mr. Kincaid for one reason and one reason only, General, and that was to help protect his life and property. We have done that, and if called upon to do so again I shall have no option but to comply. I believe Joe Tucker is the aggressor in this dirty business, and words and theories are small weapons against a determined aggressor."

"You talk like a Philadelphia lawyer, Benedict," the Fifty-four boss countered. "But you're dead wrong. I never wanted this feud and I don't want it now. That man sittin' alongside you—it's him that's full of hate, not me."

"Then why don't we try to put an end to that hatred now?" Madison said quickly. "Why don't you men shake hands and bury the past, right here and now, in this room?"

Tucker and Kincaid stared across the table at each other for a long, tense moment. The very air seemed thick with all the things that stood between these two strong men. Kincaid's face was cold and pale, and Joe Tucker scowled and rubbed his rough jaw. Then the Fifty-four man shrugged his heavy shoulders and said:

"I'm game if you are, Kincaid."

"I wouldn't shake hands with you if my life depended on it, Tucker," Kincaid said coldly.

"Hell burn it, Mr. Kincaid," Brazos said, leaning forward, "when you get a chance to pour oil on the water, why not take it?"

"I have no intention of shaking hands with a man who has caused me so much grief," Kincaid replied, speaking to Madison. "But I do want peace, General, and in an effort to achieve peace I shall give you my solemn word that if trouble breaks out again, I shall not be the instigator."

Kincaid got to his feet and picked up his hat.

"If that is not sufficient, then I can do no more."

Madison sighed, studied Kincaid and Tucker in turn, then looked down the long table at the sheriff. "Well, what do you think, Rudkin? Is this good enough?"

Barney Rudkin took his time answering. Rudkin had hoped against hope that the meeting would produce a positive result and end the range war. He felt now, as he gazed around the table, that a compromise had been reached but the root cause of the problem—the antagonism between

Kincaid and Tucker—remained untouched.

Then Rudkin's gaze shifted to Duke Benedict and Hank Brazos. Rudkin had no brief with the gun packer kind, but the events of the past two weeks had convinced him that the Anvil men had a sense of responsibility and fair play that set them poles apart from guns-for-hire like the Brands. He felt certain that the restraint Brazos and Benedict had shown had kept the feud from blossoming into all-out slaughter. Now he wondered if the truce could be honored simply because Brazos and Benedict wanted it to be so.

"I think it has a chance, General," Rudkin said finally.

"Then we shall leave it at that," Madison said. "I leave you with the sincere hope that it will not be necessary for me to bring my soldiers back to Sheridan."

Burk Kincaid gave a curt nod, fitted his hat to his head and walked to the doors. Benedict and Brazos rose, exchanged a pensive glance, and then, with a nod to Madison, followed. Stacey Blaine put a hand on Rudkin's shoulder, then went out as the Tucker group got up. Joe Tucker seemed about to say something to Madison, but walked on. Rudkin sat motionless listening to the sounds made by departing boots. Flint Brand wore big rowel spurs that jingled musically but jarred the badge-packer's ears.

Rudkin heaved his heavy bulk to his feet and Madison picked up his hat. It was pure white and high-crowned, with an ostrich feather in the brim. An identical hat had been a familiar sight on Civil War battlefields when the general had ridden at the head of his famed 8th Cavalry. Madison fluffed at the plumes with his riding quirt, then looked at the lawman.

"They would have none of my counsel," Madison intoned. "They despised all my reproof. Old Testament, Rudkin. Book of Proverbs."

Rudkin gave a grin. "You sound like Benedict, General."

Madison's blond brows came together in a frown. "Sir?"

"He's got a habit of quotin' things like that."

"Indeed? Well, I suppose that does not surprise me greatly. A most uncommon type to be found behind a six-gun, wouldn't you agree, Sheriff?"

"Reckon I would at that."

Madison sighed. "Well, did we make any ground, Sheriff?"

"Reckon we made a lot. Leastways, you did, General."

"I hope they believed my warning."

"I reckon you got it across clear enough."

With the leather riding crop bending in his hands, Madison stood before Rudkin with his booted feet wide apart, looking like a man giving an address to a multitude instead of just one large sheriff.

"There are many things wrong with the West at the moment, Rudkin, but I doubt if there is any greater evil than the nurturing of private hatreds between men of power. But right shall prevail, Sheriff Rudkin, and by heaven, I shall see that it does!"

"Sure, General, sure."

"We have a solemn duty to uphold the law, Sheriff, and I want to make it clear that I expect you to work diligently and purposefully towards the attainment of total law and order."

Rudkin flushed. "I'm doin' my best, General."

"Then do better, sir! The responsibility of this situation lies as much with you as with me, and my parting exhortation to you is to strive, with all your might, to ascertain that this fragile peace we have secured today is maintained. Good day, sir."

Rudkin was scowling heavily as he followed Madison's diminutive figure from the room. Outside, Rudkin leaned a meaty shoulder against the porch upright. Madison strode away, spoke tersely to his soldiers, then swaggered down the street with the men following.

The sheriff's face softened a little then. General Madison might be all kinds of puffed-up glory-hunter, but there was an aura about the man that made itself felt. People might laugh at Madison behind his back, and they might scoff at his puritanical habits and his theatrical way of doing things, but when it came right down to cases you just had to admire the little runt.

5

Tucker Buys

FROM the window of the Silver Dollar Saloon, Hank Brazos watched the cavalrymen ride out. They made a brave sight in their blue uniforms with General Montgomery H. Madison in the lead on his big white horse.

Dust rose behind the troopers, then settled slowly to the street, lending yet another saffron coat to the windows of the Silver Dollar already in urgent need of a wash.

The Texan took a pull on his beer and then turned back to Benedict to find him staring pensively down at his shot glass.

"Cheer up, Yank," Brazos drawled. "This is a celebration, not a wake."

Benedict lifted his eyes briefly, then looked down at his glass again. It was half an hour since the meeting had broken up. They had invited Kincaid along for a drink, but the rancher had insisted on returning immediately to the Anvil ranch with Blaine. The Silver Dollar had fallen silent upon the arrival of gunfighters but the atmosphere had returned to normal quickly once it had gotten around that an agreement had been reached between Tucker and Kincaid at the courthouse, and Brazos and Benedict were not the only ones present celebrating the peace.

Yet Duke Benedict's celebration continued to be the low-key kind.

"All right," Brazos said finally as he filled a dish with beer and put it down on the floor for Bullpup. "Get it off your chest, Yank."

Benedict looked at him absently. "Get what off my chest?"

"Whatever's been there ever since we left the meetin', of course."

"You're perceptive, Johnny Reb. Slow, but perceptive."

"What's that ten-dollar word mean?"

"It means …" Benedict swirled the liquor in his glass, then leaned back against the bar and surveyed the room. "What did you think of Tucker?"

"Big, tough. No man to walk over."

"Straight?"

"Hard to say."

"The Brands are scum."

"Not much doubt about that."

"Does it follow that the man who hires scum is no better himself?"

Brazos tugged out his makings and looked thoughtful as he began to fashion a brown-paper cigarette. "Guess it's always hard to take a clear line on somethin' like that, Benedict. A man gets up to his eyebrows in trouble and sometimes he can't be too fussy about who he gets to help him out, just as long as he gets 'em quick."

The piano started in the far corner. A drunken cowboy got up to dance with a girl in a low-cut red-spangled dress. Benedict followed the couple with his eyes, his expression still pensive.

"Kincaid could have shaken hands," he said abruptly.

"So now we're gettin' to it. That set *you* back a bit, too, did it?"

"You were surprised also?"

Brazos licked his cigarette into shape and put it in his mouth. "Tolerably surprised, I'll allow." He produced a match and lit the smoke. "I'd have liked it better if he shook hands when he had the chance. Sure got somethin' deep and hard against that Tucker, ain't he?"

"True enough. As far as I can gather, the ill-feeling dates back a long way. I sense more than know that originally it stemmed simply from the difference in the two men. Kincaid is an educated gentleman and Tucker is hardscrabble all the way."

"No call to get at one another's throats just on account of that. Look at you and me. I'm a eddicated gent and you're rough as they come, but we don't horse around shootin' at one another."

"I'm serious," Benedict said.

"Yeah, I guess I should be, too." Brazos puffed on his cigarette, then went on. "Been askin' Emma about the old days recently."

Benedict frowned briefly at mention of Emma Kincaid, for the only hand he had to hold out at the Anvil was that of the plain though interesting Sarah. But with more important things on his mind than romance, or the lack of it, Benedict said:

"I've been trying to probe Sarah and Stacey, but I haven't learned much. Have you?"

"Not much. One thing I do know, though—this feud wasn't more'n a bit of bad feelin' until about five years ago. Somethin' happened then that lit a fire. But I don't know what."

"Five years ago …" Benedict frowned. There was something he felt he should remember. *Five years* … suddenly he snapped his fingers. "That would have been about the time Kincaid's son left Anvil."

Brazos nodded. "I reckon so. And now you come to mention it, Yank, it seems to me there was somethin' mighty peculiar about that boy leavin'. Nobody wants to talk about it. I've tried to draw Emma out about her brother, but she just clams up. I can see plain she and Sarah thought the sun shone out of that boy, but they sure enough don't mean to open up on the subject."

"Kincaid and Blaine are the same," Benedict said. "I mentioned Virgil to Kincaid once and he looked at me as if I'd cursed in church. Then he just walked away."

Brazos grinned. "Must've been a real heller from what I picked up from a couple of fellers here in town. Wild as they come, so they say. Shot up a couple of hardcases here in town once. Good with a gun and horses. You'd figure he'd be the sort of son Kincaid would be right proud of."

"There could be a connection," Benedict murmured. "I'd like to really get to the bottom of it all … just to satisfy my curiosity before we leave."

Brazos looked at his partner sharply. "Ain't figurin' on pullin' out yet, are you?"

Benedict frowned. "I have high hopes that this armistice will last, but I feel we shall have to stay on for a while longer to be certain."

"Guess so," Brazos grinned slyly. "Anyway, I reckon Miss Emma would be all broke up if I was to tip my hat and say so-long this soon."

Benedict's eyes turned glacial. "The more I think about it, the more I'm forced to think there must be something critically amiss with that girl's eyesight, not to mention her taste."

"She thinks I'm good-lookin'."

"Judas!"

"And honest. Emma likes fellers she can trust. Folks don't always feel they can trust pilgrims that dress up like it was Christmas Eve every day and wear frills on their shirts."

"She said that?"

"Nope. I did."

Benedict was searching for a suitable rejoinder when the batwings swung in and Joe Tucker and his ramrod entered the saloon. A hush fell over the Silver Dollar, and several drinkers who had been standing near Benedict and Brazos, moved quickly away as the Fifty-four men ambled towards the bar.

"Whisky!" Joe Tucker said in his deep voice, slapping the bar.

Ramrod Shep Beckett watched Benedict and Brazos while they in turn looked at the batwings for a sign of the brothers Brand. The barkeep poured two whiskies. Tucker downed his with a flick of the wrist, ordered another, then stared at Benedict. Their glances met and locked. The only sound in the saloon was the loud ticking of the clock above the bar. Shep Beckett's hand shook, causing him to spill a little whisky on his shirtfront. The man swore and the sound of his voice unlocked the tension.

Benedict nodded gravely. "Tucker."

"Howdy." Joe Tucker picked up his glass, frowned thoughtfully, then glanced at them again. "Buy you a drink?"

"Never been known to turn down a free one, Tucker," Brazos grinned. He drained his glass and moved down the bar. Benedict followed slowly. He studied Tucker's face, then turned to the ramrod who had spilled his whisky.

"Relax, Mr. Beckett," Benedict said quietly. "You're among friends— as of an hour ago."

The rancher looked impressed as he passed them their drinks. "You figure on takin' the agreement serious then, do you, Benedict?"

"Don't you?"

"If I can." Tucker lifted his glass. "To better times than we've been havin'."

The spectacle of the Fifty-four boss and the Anvil gunfighters standing together drinking a toast in rye whisky held the Silver Dollar customers spellbound. Smacking his lips, Brazos turned to sweep his eyes over the staring faces.

"Well, get on with whatever you were doin'," Brazos barked. "This ain't nothin' special. Fact is, you'll likely see a whole heap more of it from now on."

"I wish I could be as sure of that as you sound, Brazos," Tucker said as the customers returned self-consciously to their whisky and cards.

"You have reservations?" Benedict asked.

"Can't help it."

"You would probably have less room for doubt if you were to get rid of that pair of butchers on your payroll, Tucker."

"The Brands ain't so bad."

"You don't sound too convincin'," Brazos observed. "They still about?"

"Nope. Sent 'em back to the spread." Tucker looked at his glass. "That Ram don't hold his likker too good."

"Nor do I, but I try my best," Benedict smiled. "Another round if you please, bartender."

With a fresh glass in hand, Joe Tucker leaned his heavy back against the bar, his old-fashioned sourdough jacket gaping open to reveal his gun. The leather shell holders on his belt were cracked and dog-eared and the gun looked ready to be pensioned off.

"Your boss never elected to stop off for a shot?" Tucker asked after a silence.

"Nope. He was anxious to get home," Brazos supplied.

Tucker stared at them soberly. "You men reckon he'll go along with Madison?"

"We don't have any cause to think otherwise," said Benedict.

The Fifty-four man took a pull on his drink, then subjected them to a long and intense scrutiny. Finally he said, "I could be wrong, I'll allow, but it seems to me that you jaspers don't fit the gunfighter stamp."

"We're not gunfighters," Benedict said firmly. "The term refers to one who kills for a living. We're simply men who at times find it necessary to use guns, or whatever other means at our disposal, to prevent injustice. There's a big difference."

"Like I said," Tucker murmured, "you don't fit. I got to figurin' you weren't the real breed after that business at Three Buttes. My men told me you could have likely chopped them all down if you had a mind, and I thank you for holdin' back. And takin' Stock into town to get him patched up, that was white of you. It's a damned pity, you know …"

"What is?" asked Brazos.

"That you're fightin' on the wrong side." Joe Tucker straightened and it was difficult to doubt the man's obvious sincerity and deep regret as he added: "You really are on the wrong side, boys. I'd have buried this feud years ago if Burk Kincaid would've let me …"

***

Restless and uneasy, Hank Brazos ground his cigarette stub under his heel and again went to the bunkhouse door to look outside for a sign of Benedict. The Yank was overdue; he should have been back from his patrol along the Fifty-four border an hour ago.

By mid-afternoon, Brazos decided he wouldn't wait any longer. Saddling his appaloosa and whistling up Bullpup who was off on one of his daily forays to the bull pen, he rode from headquarters and headed west.

The sun was warm on his face and the smell of spruce came to him as he rode the trail along Cherry Creek. Far to the south were dust clouds rising from the Five Mile branding yards. The roundup was in full progress, and with most of the hands free from sentry duty now that peace had descended over the cattle country, the cow work was progressing swiftly and Calem had told Brazos that morning that they'd be all through by the weekend.

The big horseman rode over the high hills where the sky seemed very close and the air was light. On the horizon, the Peloncillo Ranges shouldered against the sky, still holding a trace of snow.

At Cricket Gulch, Brazos reined in and searched for sign. There was any amount to be found, but none fresh. He pushed on through the jackpine forest and had just raised the tips of Three Buttes when Bullpup propped and growled. Checking his horse, Brazos pulled his Colt as he swung in the saddle to follow the line of the hound's yellow-eyed stare.

He drove his Colt back into leather with a mutter of disgust. Duke Benedict sat on a rocky shelf in the shade some two hundred yards across a draw. He had his legs crossed and his hat was tipped down over his forehead. Cigar smoke curled lazily towards his black horse which stood tethered to a mesquite clump.

The appaloosa grunted as Brazos sent him down the draw. Bullpup scampered ahead, barking menacingly. Benedict and the dog didn't get along. In Benedict, Bullpup saw the same qualities of arrogance and disdain that had made him an immediate adversary of Curway Masters Vivian the Fourth. As far as Benedict was concerned, Bullpup was just too disreputable and belligerent to warrant anything more than icy tolerance. He casually drew his right-hand gun as the dog bounded up onto the stone, showing all his teeth.

"Nice doggie," Benedict drawled. "Come to Benedict, nice doggie, and Benedict will blow your sawdust from here to Kingdom Come."

Bullpup stopped barking. He knew just how far he could go with Benedict. The hound turned his big head as Brazos rode up, as if inviting his master to witness this testimony to their unnecessary three-mile journey.

Brazos' horse pranced onto the rocky shelf, then halted, blowing air. The Texan fixed the relaxing Benedict with a baleful eye.

"What the hell do you think you're doin'? You were due back two hours ago. You knew a man'd worry."

"Why, Reb," Benedict said, getting to his feet, "if I didn't know better I'd think you really cared." He jerked a thumb at his horse. "Picked up a frog stone."

"Why didn't you get it out?"

"You know I have no talent for that sort of thing. Besides, I knew you would be along sooner or later."

Hank Brazos' craggy young face was tight as he stepped down and tugged out his clasp knife. At times like this, he felt that city-bred Benedict should never wander far from a saloon or a painted lady's bedchamber.

But as he set to work to extricate the stone from the black's forefoot, he felt his annoyance quickly fade. When Benedict had failed to show on time, he had been thinking the worst. It was better to see him there looking superior instead of finding him face-down in the grass.

It took but a few minutes to get the stone free, then Brazos went back to his saddlebags for a bottle of his special liniment. He applied it to the hoof and the black nuzzled his shoulder. Brazos rose, patted the animal's neck, then turned to Benedict with sweat trickling down from his hairline.

"You can ride him, but take it easy. Pick out the soft goin'.""

"Well done, Reb," Benedict said patronizingly as he took the reins. "Everything in order back at headquarters?"

Brazos packed his liniment away and fitted foot to stirrup. "Smooth as silk. How's the border?"

"Tranquil as a monastery garden," Benedict said from the saddle.

Brazos grunted. "Beginnin' to look like Tucker means to keep his word."

They pushed their horses off the ledge and rode slowly down the slope of the draw. "One can only trust and pray," Benedict drawled flippantly. His drowsing rest in the shade had put him in an easy mood.

Saddle leather creaked as the horses began to climb. Brazos fingered his battered hat back from his blond thatch and asked:

"You been doin' any thinkin' about what Tucker said to us the other day in Sheridan, Yank? About us workin' the wrong side of the fence, I mean."

"I rather feel that your benighted rustic daddy, with whose philosophic pronouncements you never cease to regale me, had the right idea about a matter such as that."

Brazos' brow knitted. "What's that jawbone mean?"

"It means, in your splendid raggedy-assed parent's words—too much thinkin' is liable to rot the linin' of your brain."

Brazos gave up at that. It was plain he wasn't going to get much sense out of Benedict right now. Or was Benedict being more serious than he realized? It could just be the Yank's way of telling him there was little profit to be found in delving into the matter too deeply, considering their position on the Anvil ranch.

They rode through the trees with sunlight dappling their shoulders. Birds twittered in the brush and Brazos remembered, pleasurably, that Emma had told him they would be having pot roast for supper. When they left the timber behind, Bullpup kept outstripping them, then was forced to wait impatiently until they caught up. The hound was in a hurry to get home. The bull had expertly kicked him through the second railing of the pen that morning and he was anxious to get back to even the score.

6

A Gun Too Fast

THE same bright sun that turned the Keogh County rangeland green and gold that afternoon shone hotter, whiter, on the border town of Snakebite far to the south.

Snakebite was a mean town, and the dust that gusted down the crooked little main street under the push of the wind didn't improve things any.

Even so, to the locals grouped on the porch of the battered Hardcase Hotel, it still didn't seem a good day to die, though the boy with the curly black hair and rain-colored eyes seemed bent on doing just that.

"You must be a little tetched in the haid, boy," a grizzled old veteran said from around a cud of plug tobacco. "Leastways I can't figure no feller in his right mind goin' out of his way to tangle with Kid Silk."

The boy with the thonged-down gun just laughed. His name was Billy Mack, and he couldn't take his eyes off the distant figure seated in the lacy shade of a cottonwood tree near the old well.

"You got a grudge agin the Kid?" asked another.

Mack shook his curls. "Nope. It just bothers me that any man can stand so damn tall."

The men exchanged a helpless look. They knew this kind in Snakebite; they knew the wild boys with gun smoke in their eyes who came riding in from time to time on the hunt for some big name or another. For lawless Snakebite was a haven for men of the fast gun trade. That, and a graveyard for the ambitious boys who wanted nothing more from life than to claim

55

some famous scalp, then see how they fitted a dead man's boots. Sometimes, like today, the locals tried to talk the boys out of it. But most times they just shrugged and moved away until the gun smoke cleared.

It was a thankless task, trying to talk wild boys out of dying so young.

"Well, gents," Mack grinned, hitching at his heavy shell belt. "I'll be back to buy you all a drink after I find out what the Kid is using for gut-stuffin' these days."

"Better have that drink now, boy," the old man called after him as he started off. "On account of I hear tell they're right shy on good likker in the place you're headin' for."

Billy Mack's laugh drifted back to them … and carried clearly to the well where the gunfighter sat in the shade with old Charlie Koe …

He had come by the name Kid Silk because of his penchant for wearing full-sleeved silk shirts. When he came to the border country five years ago with no name he chose to give, Kid Silk had seemed to fit. He had been a kid then, young and unlined, with a spring in his step. But five years along the wild border had left a heavy mark. He wore his fair hair shoulder-length, and his heavy, corn-colored moustache made him appear much older than his twenty-six years. The eye he had lost in a clash of Colts was covered by a black patch. The spring had gone from his step, for his right leg was stiff, legacy of the fusillade of bullets that had almost ended his life in a lawman's ambush in Arizona years ago. Only his figure was still young, lithe and supple with a narrow waist any girl might envy. A gold ring flashed on his finger as he lifted a hand to brush away a fly.

"Better move along, Charlie," he said quietly. "You don't want to stop a stray one."

The old-timer, who was one of those who liked to batten onto the famous or notorious, shook his head. "There won't be no wild ones, Kid. You'll plug the brat clean, like always."

"Maybe I'll be able to talk him out of it." But Kid Silk sneered at his own words. You could never talk them out of it.

The sound of spur chimes carried to him and Silk turned his golden head to stare at the approaching figure. Dust fogged past Mack, carried away by the hot breeze. The Kid's eye was cold, but there was a deeper coldness in his heart. He didn't want to kill the fool boy; he killed enough to earn a living without adding to the grim tally for no good reason.

A deep feeling of lassitude crept over him as Mack covered the last stretch of street to reach the well. Silk sounded bored as he spoke without looking at the boy who had drawn up with his feet wide-planted and his head held high.

"Why don't you go home and get your ma to change your diapers, son?"

Billy Mack's grin faded. Crimson stained his neck and crept over his face. "They told me you had a big mouth, Kid. Seems like they were right."

Kid Silk watched the humming flight of a dragonfly. "Did they tell you I've killed more men than the plague?"

"Bad, ain't you, Kid? Hell, you're so bad it set me to shiverin'."

He was working himself up to the pitch necessary to go for his gun. Silk had seen it so often that it was like an old book read too often.

"Go home, Mack," the Kid said.

"Can't do that. You'd better get on your feet. I want to see how tall you really are."

"I'm just middlin' size. But this gun I wear makes me taller than you'll ever get to be."

"Better get up, Kid."

Silk didn't move. He sat in profile to Mack, but now he watched the boy from the corner of his eye. Mack fidgeted and flexed his hands over his gun butt.

"Get up!" he repeated. "I won't say it again!"

The gunfighter leaned back against the stone lazily. Billy Mack went white, spat out a curse and then sent his hand driving for his gun butt.

Kid Silk palmed his Colt and shot him between the eyes. The gaping onlookers hadn't seen Silk move. All they'd seen was the bore flame from his waist, then the coiling tendril of smoke from his gun muzzle as Billy Mack fell on his back with a thud.

Kid Silk came erect, moved to the dead man, said something in a cold voice, then limped away towards the livery.

Charlie Koe was still there when the towners reached the well.

"Told him," the old graybeard said in a hushed voice.

"Told him he was gonna die."

"Never seen anybody die quicker," another said. "I thought the Kid

57

had gone to sleep afore he cut loose."

"Never seemed to give a damn afore he drew, then looked wild clear through after it was done," remarked the hotelkeeper. The man looked at Charlie Koe. "What'd he say after he shot him, Charlie?"

"Ain't dead sure," Koe replied, scratching his thatch. "But it sounded like he said, That's another one I owe you, old man.' Wonder what he meant by that?"

Nobody knew. But then, Kid Silk had always been a mystery.

***

Flint Brand hooked his thumbs in his shell belt and slouched his way down the slope from the Fifty-four ranch house. The gunfighter was edgy and there was a tight look in his eyes. Inactivity was making him nervous. He was always at his best when things were humming along. Peace to him meant about the same thing as boredom. He didn't like being bored.

His brother emerged from the bunkhouse as he approached. Ram hadn't shaved today, he noticed. Ram was getting sloppy just sitting around counting flies. Inactivity could do that to a gun packer.

"What'd he say?" Ram said. His brother had gone up to see Tucker to get their orders for the day.

"Same as yesterday and the day before," Flint growled, pacing up and down. "Relax … take it easy."

"You tell him we had more work lined up?"

"Yeah, I told him. Guess he didn't believe me though." The previous day, a member of the Yancey Grange gang had ridden in to see the Brands. The brothers had staged a few lucrative jobs with Yancey in the past. Grange had his eye on the Doonerville bank and wanted two extra guns. Yancey was resting up in the Jimcrack Hills with his bunch for a week before riding for Doonerville. The outlaw had told the Brands that they could expect a thousand dollars each if they elected to join up.

"What do you reckon, Flint?" Ram asked after watching his brother pace for another minute or so. "Do we take Yancey up on his offer and tell Tucker to go to hell?"

It was a tough decision for Flint Brand. He was getting fed up with the inaction here, and a thousand dollars a head for a bank job certainly appealed. But bank hold-ups had a nasty habit of turning sour, he reminded himself, and he wasn't at all sure that the trouble had ended here in Keogh County. They had scores to settle with Benedict and Brazos, who had made them look like hicks at Three Buttes. And if things flared up again here on the Fifty-four, then he would hate to pass up the prospect of squaring the account.

"I guess we can give it a few more days," he finally decided.

"Yeah, guess so." Ram suddenly brightened. "Of course, we could always mosey out and stir somethin' up on our lonesome, Flint. Kinda get this turkey shoot movin' again?"

"You think I ain't thought of that?" Flint shook his head. "Tucker's too smart. That's why he's keepin' us here underfoot and not lettin' us go near the border."

Ram's face fell. "In that case, you got any booze stashed?"

"You're drinkin' too much."

"What else is there?"

"Maybe you've got a point. I'll see what I've got."

***

Brad Cooley had never seen five hundred dollars at one time before, and couldn't take his eyes from the thick wad of bills lying on the desk in the pool of lamplight as Burk Kincaid talked.

"Are you sure you have it clear in your mind what I require of you now, Cooley?"

"Sure, boss."

Cooley was a heavy-set redhead with a pair of pale blue eyes set too close together over a broken nose. Prior to the arrival of Brazos and Benedict, Cooley had been classified as the Anvil's top gun. Though not in the same class as Benedict or the Brands, Cooley had proved himself a capable if unimaginative trouble-shooter. But his small star had been eclipsed by Benedict and Brazos. He didn't get on with either man and they in turn had quickly let Kincaid know that he was not the sort of gun they wanted working with them on the border. They considered Cooley likely to shoot first and think about it second. As a consequence, Cooley had spent most of his time lately either in the saddle or branding calves. He had been surprised when Kincaid had called him into his office the previous night to sound him out on a job of work worth five hundred dollars.

Cooley had been wary at first, for Kincaid's proposal was risky. He had told the Anvil boss he would sleep on it. He did just that, and he'd awakened this morning knowing he simply couldn't afford to pass up the offer. A man could live high and go a long way on five hundred, and after the job was done Brad Cooley planned to do just that. He'd had enough of Anvil, and more than enough of Benedict and Brazos.

"If anything goes wrong, Cooley," Kincaid said now, rising, "you're on your own. I know nothing. As far as I'm concerned you pulled your time and left. Is that clear?"

"Sure is. Can I have the dinero now, Mr. Kincaid?"

Kincaid gestured at the money and then he walked across to his window that overlooked the courtyard. Fingering the curtain aside, he looked out to see the servants putting the finishing touches to the preparations for the night's festivities. It was Saturday night and they had finished the roundup yesterday. The idea of throwing a roundup party had been his daughters'. The rancher had not thought much of the idea, but in the end he'd given his permission. The house had been in bedlam all day and he'd lost count of the number of times he had had to call for quiet while he worked over the books.

Cooley ranged up beside him and looked out. "Kind of sorry I'll miss the wingding, Mr. Kincaid. Looks like bein' a good one."

Kincaid let the curtain fall. "It's time you were gone, Cooley."

"Guess so, boss. Well …" Cooley thrust out his hand, but Kincaid didn't seem to see it. The rancher walked to his desk and spoke with his back to the man.

"Goodbye, Cooley."

"So long, boss."

Kincaid didn't turn until the door had closed on Cooley's back. He rested the heels of his hands on the desk edge and stared at nothing. Above the noise from the courtyard, he heard Curway Masters Vivian give tongue. The cattleman's head turned from side to side as if to ward off unwelcome thoughts. He had fifteen thousand acres of the best cattle country in Nevada. And he'd paid two thousand dollars for a bull to make his the best herd in the country.

And for what? There was no one to leave it to except two girls who would probably marry fortune-hunters. There was no son to take it over and carry on the name.

And it was all their fault … Tucker and his daughter. How could a man help but hate them?

He moved slowly to the whisky cabinet and poured himself a heavy drink. He lifted his glass in a bitter salutation to the past, and as if that were a signal, a guitar started to thrum in the yard.

The big night was getting under way.

***

"You really do dance beautifully, Duke," Emma Kincaid smiled as they circled under the paper lanterns to the music of a tired guitar.

"At last," smiled Benedict.

"At last what, Duke?"

"Why, at last the wench has found something about her humble servant to admire."

Emma's laugh was gay. *"You* humble, Duke Benedict? I don't believe I've ever met a less humble man. But you're nice—much nicer than I thought at first."

"Ah, let me hear more, dear lady. For words fitly spoken are like apples of gold in a picture of silver."

"You want words, Duke?" called Jim Crocker, wearily plunking his steel guitar. "I'll give you two. I'm beat."

"Head for the blankets then, Jim," called Brazos, standing off to one side with Sarah, Blaine and Curly Calem. He lifted his harmonica. "I'll wear 'em out with this."

"Wear *us* out you mean," Curly Calem said, striding towards Benedict and Emma. "I'm cuttin' in, Duke."

"Over my dead body," Benedict smiled, then he scowled as Emma slipped from his arms and held out her hands to the cowhand. "Well, I'll be damned," he muttered as Brazos struck up a lively tune. He turned and bowed to Stacey Blaine. "May I have the pleasure?"

"Sorry, I'm all booked up," the ramrod laughed, and went twirling away with Sarah.

Benedict struck a mock tragic pose in the center of the courtyard, then headed for the improvised bar where a sleepy servant nodded over the bottles.

"Give strong drink unto him that is ready to perish, and wine unto those that be heavy of heart," he ordered, chucking the girl under the chin. "Interpretation? One very large whisky, my child, then off to bed with you." His brows went up. "Alone?" His brows went down again. "Yes, regrettably, alone." Duke Benedict wasn't drunk, but he was filled with rare high spirits. It had been that sort of a night. With the roundup behind them, the hands had entered into the spirit of the party with gusto. The music had been fast and the dancing spectacular, with not one jarring note between eight p.m. and almost three in the morning.

The jarring note came a half hour later, when the hard core of survivors trooped out noisily to settle a pre-dawn difference of opinion between a noisy stud bull and the indefatigable Bullpup. But when it struck it hit stunningly hard.

Zeke Hanlon rode in astride a lathered horse almost run off its feet. There had been gunplay on the Fifty-four. Fifty-four hand Jack Carrol, who was Hanlon's cousin, had brought the stunning news to Hanlon's lookout position an hour ago.

Carrol had said three men had been killed on Fifty-four ground along Whipple Creek. Two of the dead were Fifty-four hands. The third man was Anvil rider, Brad Cooley.

The two days that followed the gun battle at Whipple Creek were the most difficult and dangerous Benedict and Brazos had put in since coming to Anvil. For in the maelstrom of fury stirred up by the apparently senseless outbreak of violence, they seemed to be alone in trying to keep the incident from erupting into a full-blooded war.

Several men from both sides were wounded in clashes following the Whipple Creek affair, but nobody was killed—thanks to Brazos and Benedict who seemed to be everywhere along the border, ready to intervene at the first crash of shots.

Mystery surrounded the Whipple Creek incident. Apparently a rifleman had opened up on the sleeping Fifty-four camp and two hands had been killed in their blankets. The sniper had then taken to his heels, but the pursuing Fifty-four men had caught up when his horse broke a leg in a gopher hole on the ranch's west border. They shot the sniper down and the man turned out to be Brad Cooley. Cooley had five hundred dollars on him, and on his horse was a bedroll.

Why had Cooley embarked on such a course of action?

Nobody seemed to know, but Brazos and Benedict were doing their weary best to find out late that second afternoon when General Montgomery H. Madison and a squad of troopers descended on Anvil headquarters in a blue swarm.

The general was in no mood to listen to reason. He had received a report on the fresh outbreak of trouble while on the trail of the Piute renegade. Many Kills, in the Dallas Mountains, and he considered it probable now that the Indian killer would escape. So, angry and frustrated, he told all who would listen that he'd given clear warning as to his course of action in the event of a breach of the peace.

He would arrest Benedict, Brazos and the Brand brothers.

And if that didn't put an end to the bloodshed, then by thunder he might arrest every man on the Fifty-four and Anvil and herd them up to the State penitentiary and to hell with the consequences!

Benedict protested vehemently against what he considered to be the foolish and dangerous step of taking them out of the firing line, but when he and Brazos saw that Madison was adamant, they had no choice but to turn in their guns, after extracting a promise that Madison would post troops between the Fifty-four and Anvil ranches to maintain order.

The Brand brothers were picked up at about the same time when a score of soldiers arrived suddenly at Three Buttes. Flint Brand was enraged at the turn of events, but satisfied himself with only verbal resistance. However, big Ram took a punch at a trooper and arrived at the Sheridan jailhouse two hours later sporting a black eye and a missing tooth.

Sundown saw an uneasy peace settle once more over troubled Keogh County.

7

Jailhouse Blues

"WHY?" General Madison barked yet again as he paced the law office banging his saddle whip against his boot top. "Why did that Cooley jackanapes attack? Why?"

"I've asked myself that more times than I can recall, General," Barney Rudkin said from the depths of his horsehair-stuffed chair. "It doesn't make sense."

"Men don't usually commit acts of wanton lawlessness without some reason, sir. Is it possible that Cooley harbored a private enmity against the Fifty-four which he attempted to settle after leaving Kincaid's employ?"

"Not that I know of."

"And you don't know how he came by that five hundred dollars?"

"Nope. Nobody on Anvil seems to know either. They all said Cooley spent his money as fast as he got it."

Madison halted in the doorway. His back was slightly stooped, a sign that the general was exhausted, for he liked to boast that he had been adjudged to have had the straightest back in West Point Academy.

Deputy Eli Peachman caught the sheriff's eye and angled, his head at the coffee pot seated on the stove. Rudkin nodded and the deputy got up to pour him a mug. From the cell-block came the sound of a softly played harmonica. Madison cocked his head at the sound of the music and turned, wearing an uncharacteristic expression of confusion.

"Confounded awkward situation, Rudkin!"

"How's that, General?"

"That fellow Brazos. And Benedict. It seems patently clear to me now that they and perhaps they alone struggled mightily to maintain some semblance of sanity in this murderous affair. Hardly a fitting reward, throwing them into jail, is it?"

"You can always let 'em out, General. I don't reckon they should be in there myself."

"Can't be done, sir."

"Why not?"

"You can't make fish of one and fowl of another in a situation of this kind, sir. If we released them and not the Brands, then Tucker would have no option but to believe that the law has aligned itself against him. He would feel threatened, with his guns spiked and Brazos and Benedict back on the Anvil ranch. Almost certainly he would feel the need to bring in more gunmen, or take some other equally disastrous step."

"Yeah, I guess he would. And there wouldn't be much point in loosin' 'em *all* now that you've gone to the trouble of bringin' 'em in."

"I don't really wish to release those felonious brothers until I am forced to."

"How long do you expect that to be, General?"

Madison shook his head. "I don't really know," he said wearily. "I'd certainly relish putting the Brands where they belong, but I don't see how I can do that without treating Benedict and Brazos the same way. Originally I aligned Benedict and Brazos with the Brands and was prepared to lump them all together. It was no idle boast of mine when I said they would all be sent to prison in the event of further outbreaks. I meant it. But now …" Madison spread out his hands.

"I reckon you're anxious to get back to chasin' Many Kills, General," the sheriff said after a silence.

Weary as he was, Madison's gimlet eye brightened at mention of his old Piute adversary. There had been a running battle between. Flash Madison and the redskin renegade over the past year with honors roughly even. It had been difficult for Madison to interrupt his close pursuit of the notorious Piute to come to Keogh County.

"Anxious is too small a word, Sheriff," he declared. "I propose to leave at first light and resume pursuit of the heathen malefactor. I feel quite certain he is making for their summer stronghold in Horsehead Mountain. I plan to set up a base camp and conduct a systematic campaign …"

Madison paused and glanced at the archway leading into the cell-block. Hank Brazos, whether by accident or design, was now playing *Garry Owen.* It was the marching song of Madison's Civil War regiment, the 8th Cavalry.

The general rose suddenly.

"Enough shillyshallying, Rudkin," he barked. "A firm decision must be made and made now. Perhaps, with the Brands and Benedict and Brazos out of the picture, and my small force present on the border out there, the fighting will cease. I've gone to great trouble to bring these gunfighters in, so we must make as much capital of that as possible."

The general looked at Rudkin directly.

"Hold the four of them for one week, Sheriff Rudkin. Officially you shall charge them with disturbing the peace, but unofficially you shall be holding them pending trial for inciting to riot—a far more serious matter. Let them and their employers believe they are in the very deepest trouble. It could well be that this will have such a sobering effect that all four, when they are released at week's end, shall decide they've had enough of this business and pull out. Do you approve?"

The very fact that Madison sought his opinion was proof to the lawman that the general lacked his normal confidence. But Rudkin, after considering the general's proposal, felt more positive.

"I think it's a good idea, General," he declared, and he meant it. "It could take the heat out of the whole affair, and as you say it might force the gun packers to quit. With them gone, I can handle Tucker and Kincaid, just like I was doin' 'fore they brought in their hired guns."

"So be it," Madison replied, and without another word he marched into the night.

The sheriff shook his head, then turned to the cell archway. He might as well break the news to the prisoners now, he thought. Then, conjuring up a mental picture of how the four dangerous men were bound to react when they discovered they "might" be tried and sent to prison, he walked instead to the cabinet where he kept his whisky.

First, a couple of really stiff shots.
Then he would tell them.

***

The light that had burned all night in the cell corridor faded as daylight came stealing through the steel bars.

On the wall by the window where Hank Brazos stood matching the dawn, someone who had checked out long ago had scratched:

Young Tommy Burton
went east and then west,
He went the way,
he thought was best,
He thought his girl would wait.
But she didn't.

Brazos couldn't read, but he'd had Benedict recite it for him last night. "Doggerel," Benedict had said. Brazos reckoned it wasn't great poetry, but it had a feel to it. He found himself thinking about poor Tommy Burton, and he wished his girl had waited for him. But maybe Tommy could have wound up lucky after all, he thought with characteristic optimism. Could be that the girl who hadn't waited had become fat and bad-tempered. Could be that Tommy finally found himself another girl—a good one.

Pleased with his thoughts, the Texan tugged out his tobacco to roll his first cigarette of the day. The gray light from the window' put a steely hue on his broad, saddle-brown face and thick, corded hands. The purple shirt, faded from too many river washings, was unbuttoned to the waist to reveal his iron-ribbed barrel of a chest. Refreshed from a good night's sleep, he looked, under his banner of thick yellow hair, like a great overgrown boy.

The jailhouse was stirring now. Out in the front office, the deputy brewed coffee. Peachman had stood the night watch, and he yawned mightily as he stood at the pot-bellied stove with his suspenders hanging loose.

Sounds drifted in: the chirrup of birds in the cottonwoods; the creak of the water carrier's cart on its way to the river; a window banged open and an early-rising housewife flapped a mat.

Duke Benedict turned restlessly on his hard bunk, then he opened his eyes.

In the cell across the corridor, Ram Brand snored, his battered face almost covered by a gray blanket. His lean brother paced the cell, chain-smoking. Ram Brand's stupidity had landed him inside a cell many times in the past. He was used to it and it didn't bother him unduly. But his brother was different. The longer Flint Brand was locked up, the more he got to feel that the stone and steel were closing in on him, crushing his bones, pressing down on his lungs so he couldn't breathe.

Benedict was seated on the edge of his bunk pulling on his thirty-dollar boots when the deputy came through with a tray of coffee.

"Mornin', boys."

"Break a leg," said Flint Brand.

"Open a vein," snarled Ram, blinking awake.

"You sure make lousy coffee, Deputy," said Brazos after taking a taste.

But Duke Benedict just stared at the deputy in a cold way that good-natured Eli found infinitely more disturbing than the insults.

"Sleep well, Mr. Benedict?" the lawman asked hopefully as he thrust his pannikin through the bars.

"He slept all goddamn night," Flint Brand said sourly. "Must be used to bein' behind bars is all I can say."

"Where's Rudkin?" asked Benedict, ignoring Flint.

"Ain't showed yet," Peachman answered. He grinned. "Sheriff ain't a great one for early risin'."

"Then where's that army glory-hunter?"

"The general?" Peachman said. "Heck, he's been long gone, Mr. Benedict. Rode out afore dawn to get after Man Kills again."

"I want to see that bloated sheriff the moment he arrives," Benedict said, and turned his back.

The deputy sent a worried look at Brazos and then started off for the office again. "Breakfast in about an hour, gents," he called back. "We've got to wait for the cafe to open."

Silence descended, the sort of thick silence that comes to jailhouses.

The prisoners drank their coffee and brooded glumly on their prospects. Last night, Rudkin had told them they were to be charged with inciting to riot. It was a charge which, if proven, could fetch sentences of up to two years in the State penitentiary.

Breakfast proved to be about the standard of the deputy's coffee.

Rudkin came in after nine, but he didn't seem too impressed by Benedict's vehement insistence that they should be granted bail. "Can't afford to let you boys loose for fear you'll get back to shootin' at one another, Benedict," he said, then he trudged off to get his own breakfast. The lawman took his meals at the hotel. He wouldn't eat cafe fare if he got it free.

Hank Brazos worked a morsel of food from a tooth and began to croon:

"Like to get ridin, but it ain't no use,
Jailer-man won't turn me loose."

The day wore on. Around midday, Joe Tucker came in to see the Brands. After his visit, the Fifty-four boss had a noisy argument with the sheriff.

Lunch was Mulligan stew and pone bread. Brazos ate both his and Benedict's, Benedict deciding then and there to subsist on coffee and cigars.

They waited for Burk Kincaid to come in, but he didn't show.

"Most likely busy workin' on gettin' us out of here, Yank," Brazos said in the late afternoon.

"Undoubtedly." Benedict's tone was skeptical. He sat on his bunk, his left hand around the silk sleeve of his shirt above the right wrist. His fingers traced the smooth outline of the two-shot Derringer in its soft leather spring holster. The troopers and the lawmen had failed to detect the sneak gun when they searched him. With his abiding respect for the law, he was loathe to use the secret two-shot—but he would, rather than step through the gates of the State prison.

Kincaid finally appeared in the late afternoon and with him were his daughters. Kincaid said he was working to get them out, but he admitted that Barney Rudkin was proving singularly stubborn.

That was the bad news. The good news was that all was quiet out at the spread. Madison had left ten troopers at the border, and both the Anvil and Fifty-four riders had withdrawn from the area.

No he hadn't learned anything more about Brad Cooley and his attack on the Fifty-four. It remained a mystery.

Dusk settled quickly over Sheridan when the Anvil party had left the jailhouse. Supper—and a visitor for the Brands—arrived at nightfall.

The Brands' visitor was a thick-set young man in a low-crowned gray hat and big spurs. He gave his name as Jackson, and though they tried to conceal it, the gunfighters were obviously delighted to see him. The three talked in low tones at the cell door for a long time, with the sheriff standing in the archway, watching.

When the man finally left and Rudkin had returned to his chair, the Brands sat on their bunks and talked in whispers, grinning broadly.

Two sober men watched from the opposite cell. The Brands were definitely not the smiling kind. What could Jackson have told them to put them in such high spirits?

Of course, they had no way of knowing—nor did they know the name of the man in the gray hat and big spurs was not Jackson, but Yodie Monroe.

Yodie Monroe was an outlaw. He rode with the Yancey Grange gang. And Yancey Grange was a friend of the Brand brothers from way back.

Sleep was slow in coming that night.

Brazos dozed off first around eleven. His early sleep was troubled by bad dreams that were dimly connected with the range war. But finally, after a great deal of tossing and turning, he drifted into a deep and dreamless sleep.

It took Duke Benedict a lot longer to find the solace of sleep. Havanas continued to lend the cell their fragrance until well after midnight. There were too many uncertainties, mysteries and loose ends on Duke's mind to let him rest easily. There were so many things he didn't understand—like the way Joe Tucker had looked that day in the saloon when he told them they were fighting on the wrong side. And the mystery that surrounded Kincaid's son; he sensed that much hinged on Virgil Kincaid, but the subject was a blank wall. The biggest puzzle of all, of course, was Burk Kincaid himself. He was intelligent, impressive, a fine figure of a man. But there was something locked inside Kincaid that wouldn't let the man unbend. He seemed ever on his guard, as though afraid to reveal something he had to keep hidden.

And there was Cooley.

Every time Benedict thought about Brad Cooley, he frowned. He hadn't liked the man from the beginning. Both he and Brazos had tabbed him as a breed they despised, a small-time gunfighter without principle. They had eased the man out of the Anvil fighting force for that very reason, and they'd been happy to hear he was leaving the Anvil. It was obvious that somebody had paid Cooley the five hundred to attack the Fifty-four muster camp. But who? And even more confounding—why?

Questions without end, and no answers worth a damn.

Benedict stubbed out his last cigar and took his thoughts to bed.

***

Hank Brazos didn't know what had awakened him. It was near morning. He heard Benedict's deep, even breathing from across the cell. He was tempted to turn his head and look across at the Brands, but something restrained him.

He waited.

Then it came—a furtive whisper from across the stone corridor.

Every sense intensely alert now, the Texan lay motionless under his blanket. The faint sound of a knock came from the front of the building. He heard the deputy stir, then his sleepy, muffled voice. Another knock. Bed springs creaked. Footsteps.

The sound of a door bolt being drawn. A sudden gasp, then a sharp thud followed by a heavier one.

Brazos felt his heart skip and then beat a little faster. Metal rasped against metal in the front office. He held his breath at the sound of a quick, light step in the corridor.

A figure came into sight under the night lamp. Short, stocky, under a gray hat.

Jackson!

Brazos looked at Benedict's bunk. The Yank was awake. Then he turned his head to see Jackson at the door of the next cell. The gunmen were whispering excitedly. Brazos made to swing his feet to the floor, but Benedict threw him a warning gesture. Brazos swore under his breath. They couldn't just sit back and let the hellions break out. The least they could do was kick up a racket to raise the alarm. Again he started to move, but Benedict said:

"No!"

Then Brazos caught the gleam of metal in Benedict's right hand. He sucked in a huge breath. He'd forgotten the sneak gun.

The Brands' door swung open.

"I'm here to tell you that we ain't never gonna forget this, Yodie," Flint Brand whispered. He stepped out and Yodie Monroe backed to within a foot of the opposite cell.

Duke Benedict came out of his bunk like a striking panther. Leaping to the door, he plunged his left arm through the bars, whipped his forearm across the outlaw's neck, then jerked his back viciously against the bars and stabbed the muzzle of the deadly two-shot into his backbone.

Yodie Monroe made a strangled sound. The Brands gaped in astonishment that quickly turned to fury.

"You dirty bastard, Benedict!" Flint Brand snarled, but the choked, bug-eyed Monroe cut him off:

"No, Flint! He's got a gun in my back!"

"Stay put!" Benedict snapped at the Brands. "Reb, get the keys from this man, pronto."

As Brazos drove his hand through the bars to seize Monroe's right arm, Ram Brand lunged at him. Brazos jerked Monroe's arm back against the door then slammed his left fist through the bars at Ram's contorted face. As Ram staggered back, Flint grabbed him by the shoulder and propelled him towards the office.

"We need guns, Ram!"

"Hold!" Benedict yelled.

But the Brands kept running. Duke whipped the derringer from Monroe's back and fired. Ram Brand staggered as the crash of the shot filled the jailhouse, but he kept his feet to vanish through the archway after his brother.

"Quick, Reb!" Benedict shouted, plucking Monroe's six-gun from his belt. "Get it open before they get their hands on guns out there and come back shooting!"

73

But the Brand brothers didn't return. Benedict's shot had sounded as loud as the crack of doom to the desperate gunfighters. To re-enter the cell-block and face down Brazos and Benedict simply because they had taken Yodie Monroe could mean a fatal delay. Yodie Monroe wasn't worth it.

Brazos and Benedict heard the Brands run out and cross the jailhouse porch as Brazos unlocked the cell door. The Texan put his shoulder to the bars and flung the door wide, sending the dazed Monroe flying across the corridor. Two long strides carried Brazos to him. A big fist swung and Monroe fell in a heap through the open door of the Brands' cell.

Benedict was already dashing for the law office as Brazos straightened. The Texan pounded after him, then flung himself at the desk as Benedict sped through the door. Grasping a Colt, Brazos skittered around the desk and hurtled out to the porch. Benedict stood in the middle of the street.

"Brands!" Benedict's voice cracked out. "Hold fast or you're dead!"

Flint Brand spun and fired. The slug whispered past Benedict's dark head.

Brazos and Benedict triggered together, twin stabs of bore-flame arrowing at the hunched figure of Flint Brand, for one glance had shown them that Ram Brand was unsteady on his feet from Benedict's quick shot in the jailhouse.

With the gun crashes echoing from the false fronts in deafening waves of sound, Flint Brand ducked to make a smaller target, then his Colt answered. At the same time big Ram got his gun working. Brazos flung himself to one side as lead stitched the corner clapboards of the law office.

Both Brazos and Benedict were down now, firing from ground level. A bullet hit the porch boards in front of the sprawled Texan, sending splinters into his chest. He winced, squeezed off another shot, then saw Flint Brand stagger as Benedict's Colt bucked again.

Flint Brand staggered, then began to run. Ram limped after him, both men firing over their shoulders. Brazos and Benedict bounded to their feet and sprinted after them. The street was thick with gun smoke. Ram Brand fell, got up and fell again. Flint whirled back towards his brother, his bloodstained shirt a crimson target in the eerie light. He screamed and staggered as the guns of Benedict and Brazos roared again.

Suddenly the guns fell silent, and the towners who had watched the bloody showdown crept cautiously from their doors.

When the gun smoke finally cleared, Flint Brand lay huddled by the saloon hitchrack, and his brother was sprawled in death in the middle of the street.

Brazos and Benedict had won.

Their fast guns had again carried the day. But the killing was far from over. The worst was yet to come.

8

Victory of a Kind

H<small>ANK</small> B<small>RAZOS</small> and Duke Benedict remained in Sheridan while Sheriff Rudkin made contact with General Montgomery Madison in the south. There was an exchange of wires between the law office and the town of Crackerville where the soldiers were resting up prior to their campaign in the Dallas Mountains.

Madison was appalled at what had transpired in Sheridan, but he displayed no hesitation in agreeing with Rudkin's insistence that Brazos and Benedict be set free. The men had risked their lives to prevent a jailbreak, and Madison was even moved to send them his thanks. Before leaving Sheridan, the general had said he didn't wish any distinction to be shown between the Fifty-four and the Anvil. This no longer applied. Two men in Tucker's employ had flouted the law, and Tucker was tainted by implication.

The general made his attitude quite plain. The Fifty-four had been seriously weakened by the loss of its gunfighters. Now it was Rudkin's duty to see that it didn't get up off its knees again. The general declared that the breakout had established Tucker as the more guilty of the two feuding parties.

"Looks like you've won, gents," the sheriff told Benedict and Brazos late one afternoon, showing them Madison's lengthy wire.

"Oh, we're natural-born winners and no mistake, Sheriff," Duke Benedict said caustically. "Come on, Reb, time to ride."

"We goin' back to the Anvil, Yank?"

"Yes."

"Don't you think mebbe it'd be best if we just kept ridin'?"

"We'll ride out only when we know it's at an end, not before."

Hank Brazos sighed. At times like this he couldn't help but think how uncomplicated life had been when he was a simple Texas cowpoke.

"Reckon as how you're right," he said finally, and went off to get the horses.

***

Joe Tucker sat in his big chair on the Fifty-four ranch house porch. His land stretched all the way down the hot valley, acre upon acre all the way to the mountains, broken here and there by the sharp upthrusts of tall, rocky buttes that rose like islands in the grassland.

Only the man's eyes moved as he sat sprawled, like a massive, careless sculpture, big head angled forward, thick legs encased in calf-length moccasins thrust out before him. From the clenched right fist that rested on the chair arm protruded the crushed end of a yellow telegraph slip.

Inside the house, Cass Tucker worked in the kitchen. From time to time she would come to the door, glance with concern at her father, then return to her chores. Cass noticed that since the death of the Brands a week earlier, her father had taken more to sitting and brooding and less to riding and working. And each day, she watched the lines in his face grow deeper.

Tucker's eyes flickered now as two horsemen came in from the west, sending plumes of dust into the sky. They were new men, Gilroy and Jones. Greenhorns. He was hiring anyone he could get these days. Over half his men had left after the Brands had been killed. They had been afraid of the repercussions, but as things turned out there had been no need. Ever since the shoot up in Sheridan, the cow country had been quiet. So quiet, in fact, that the ten troopers Madison had left behind to watch the border had ridden out yesterday to join the general in the Dallas Mountains.

But Joe Tucker knew it wouldn't stay quiet. Kincaid was content to gloat over his victory for the time being, but sooner or later he would lash out again. He would start it all up once more, and this time he would have those slick gunfighters of his, with no more opposition on the Fifty-four than a bunch of scared hands and a few greenhorns.

His hand opened slowly and he stared down at the wire. It had been brought out by mail rider Corey Jeans just that morning. Tucker hadn't moved from his chair since reading it. Now, as if it cost him great physical effort, he slowly opened the crushed note and scanned it again with a bleak eye:

> HEAR YOU ARE HAVING HARD TIMES.
> WILLING TO WORK FOR YOU IF YOU WANT.
> NO FEE.
> KID SILK.
> HARDCASE HOTEL, SNAKEBITE.

It still didn't make sense to Joe Tucker. Why should a man of Kid Silk's reputation offer his gun without pay? When Tucker had first decided to hire trouble-shooters, he had made enquiries about the notorious Silk, but had passed him over upon learning how much it would cost to secure his services.

He read the message through several times. Then, with sudden decision he turned his head and called:

"Daughter! Bring me paper and pen!"

***

"Please say we can go, Father," pretty Emma urged. "We could make a party—Sarah, Duke, Hank and I, and of course Curly and Stacey and—"

"Another dance?" Burk Kincaid said. "Good heavens, child, we had our own dance here two weeks ago. Why ...?"

"But the Summer Ball in Sheridan is always such fun, Father," Sarah cut him off. "We missed the ball last year because of trouble with the Fifty-four and we would love to go this year. Everybody will be there. And with Hank and Duke leaving soon, it would be an ideal opportunity for us to show them how much we appreciate all they have done."

"Have they said when they'll be leaving?" Kincaid asked sharply.

"Not exactly. But I can see the signs. Duke is growing restless, and so is Hank." Emma looked wistful. "I hate to think how much I'll miss Hank.

He's so kind and gentle and—"

"Has Benedict given you any firm indication when he intends leaving?" Kincaid cut in, looking at Sarah.

Sarah shook her head. "Nothing definite, Father. But, like Emma, I know it will be soon. Duke feels he's no longer needed here. I think they'll make up their minds all of a sudden when they do. And that's why it's important that we have one last night together, all of us, just for them. Surely you agree, Father?"

The cattleman frowned. "I never was much for balls. Big, noisy affairs they are …" He broke off when he saw their disappointment. It made him realize how little he ever did for his daughters. He sighed and leaned back in his study chair. "Oh, very well. And now will you kindly leave me to get on with my work?"

Moments later a broad smile broke over his face. It was worth giving in, just to see their excitement as they rushed out to tell Brazos and Benedict the news. They were good girls; never gave him a minute's trouble. Not like …

He shut off that train of thought and got up to move to the window overlooking the yard. He saw Emma running towards the barn where Hank Brazos squatted in the shade rubbing liniment on his dog. The ugly hound had tangled with Vivian again that morning and had come off a bad second.

Kincaid watched with a remote expression as Brazos got to his feet and spoke to Emma. He was a simple giant with simple ideas of right and wrong, Kincaid reflected. Not like Benedict. Duke Benedict was clever and sophisticated. Too clever? Kincaid chewed over that one. He wasn't certain how much Benedict knew or suspected. There were times when he caught Benedict studying him through those clear gray eyes of his in a way that made Kincaid feel uneasy. He wasn't at all sure that Benedict trusted him. And that was going to make his next step that much more difficult.

The next step of course, was another attack on the Fifty-four. Kincaid had been content to let things drift along for a time following the smashing victory over the Brands. But Tucker still had a price to pay, and Kincaid would never be in a better position to exact that price than while he still had Duke Benedict and Hank Brazos on his payroll.

Soon, quite soon, he would have to engineer another incident that would set the range war going again. But he would have to be careful because of Benedict and his sharp eye. The fellow had such impossibly high standards hiding behind his flashy exterior that Kincaid knew he could find himself in serious trouble if Benedict were to discover how he pulled the strings.

It might be wise to wait until after the ball on Saturday night, he decided. That would give him time to lay his plans. Sunday morning might well prove the ideal moment to stage the next play, with everybody sleeping in after the night out …

His head began to ache the way it always did when he thought about the Tuckers and what they had cost him. A vein beat in his forehead and gray fingers seemed to shadow his brain. Soon the stomach cramps would come and he would have to resort to laudanum and whisky …

A little unsteady on his feet, Kincaid made his way back to his desk. He sat down heavily and rested his face in his hands. His shoulders shook and he felt the sweat run down his backbone. Burk Kincaid had read a long time ago that hatred was a poison like any other poison you bought at a store. The only difference was that it took longer to kill you.

At times like this he always remembered what he'd read … and he wondered, a little fearfully, if it could be true …

***

Sarah Kincaid found Duke Benedict seated on the shadowed eastern gallery of the ranch house reading one of the big, buckram-bound books from her father's library.

He didn't hear her as she appeared around the verandah corner, and she halted silently, watching him.

He was the most beautiful man she had ever seen. She knew men were not supposed to be beautiful, but no other word seemed to suit Duke Benedict. Perhaps it was because of her plainness that she was so conscious of physical perfection in others. That was where she was different from Emma. Being so pretty herself, Emma didn't place so much importance on a person's appearance. She had proved that by the way she had taken such an interest in Hank Brazos. Not that Hank wasn't attractive—he was boyish and rugged and Sarah just loved to see him walking about the homestead with those huge shoulders and narrow hips. But he wasn't beautiful like Duke …

Suddenly Benedict sensed a presence and glanced up. He smiled when he saw her, but Sarah didn't fail to notice the way his hand had dropped to his gun butt first.

It sobered her, the little action that illustrated so sharply the difference between this handsome, polished man and all the other men she knew. Duke Benedict was a gunfighter. He hated the term and was ever ready to deny that he belonged to that class, but his skill with weapons lifted him from the ranks of ordinary men, and Sarah was wise enough to know that men with his abilities were never permitted to lead peaceful lives, no matter how much they might wish it. But the bad moment passed and Sarah hurried along the tiles to tell Benedict the news. As dangerous as Duke Benedict was, he'd come to fill a lonely corner of her life and she would miss him terribly when he had gone.

Benedict wasn't as pleased about the arrangements for the ball as Sarah had expected. Saturday was still several days away, he pointed out. He wasn't certain that he and Brazos would still be here on the ranch.

But having just spent considerable time and effort in persuading her father to attend the ball, Sarah was not about to give up easily on the guests of honor. She told him what the Summer Ball was like, about the pretty girls and the music—and how upset she and Emma would be if Benedict and Brazos didn't attend.

Smiling then at Sarah's excitement, Benedict agreed to talk to Brazos and see what his thoughts were.

Brazos and Emma were both rubbing liniment into Bullpup's leathery hide when Sarah and Benedict reached the barn. The dog lay on his side on a canvas-covered bench, lapping up all the attention. His pink tongue lolled and he looked weary—but not so much so that he wasn't up to welcoming Benedict with a low growl in his deep chest.

"Ever considered rubbing some of that wonder medication of yours into the head area, Reb?" Benedict suggested. "I feel strongly that that's where the main problem lies." He winked at Sarah. "It is my considered opinion that a ninety-pound dog which persistently pits itself against a two-thousand-pound stud bull must have something seriously amiss with its mental processes."

Bullpup growled again, as if he understood. But Brazos just grinned.

"It's only on account of he's a Texan, Yank. A Texan just don't know the meaning of the word quit."

"Well, I think it's about time he thought about quitting. Hank," said Emma. "Are you sure he doesn't have any broken ribs?"

"No, he's fine, Emma," Brazos insisted, stepping back from the dog. "You just watch." He snapped his fingers and said, "Cats!"

Bullpup bounded up, hit the ground running and scooted to the end of the barn. There he halted, glowering and sniffing as his yellow eyes swept the area. Even Benedict had to laugh at the look of heavy reproof with which the hound favored his master when he realized it was a false alarm.

"Like I said," Brazos chuckled, screwing the cap on his liniment bottle, "pure Texan."

"Which is the same as pure—" Benedict began, but broke off in deference to the girls. He turned serious as he reached for his cigars. "Reb, has Emma told you about the ball?"

"Yep."

"Well, I told Sarah that I'm not at all certain we shall be able to go—"

"We're goin'."

"What?"

"I told Emma we're goin'. Matter of fact, I'm ridin' into town tomorrow to buy a new shirt."

"You made this decision without consulting me?"

"Correct." Brazos propped a big boot on the bench and thumbed his hat back. He eyed his partner challengingly.

Benedict knew that look. It meant Hank Brazos had made up his mind about something, and once that happened there was no changing it.

"In that case," Benedict said, turning to Sarah, "I suppose I had better see if I can borrow a dinner suit from your father."

The girls were delighted, and Sarah even kissed them both before she and Emma hurried off.

Brazos shook his head and grinned, as he watched them cross the yard. "Fine pair of gals that, Yank."

Benedict lit a cigar. Now that the decision about the dance had been taken out of his hands, he realized he was looking forward to it. "They are indeed that, Johnny Reb." He drew the smoke deep, looking thoughtful. "Strange, you know … when we first met the girls, I had eyes only for Emma, but over the weeks I must confess I've come to find qualities in Sarah that genuinely attract me. It may sound like sour grapes, of course, but I've reached the point where I'm more interested in her than in your Emma."

"Hell, she ain't mine."

"She acts as though she would like to be."

"You and me—we're just new, Benedict. They were used to havin' Stacey and Curly around, and when we came ridin' in—two trouble-shooters who were gonna put everythin' right in jig time—why, we were just bound to cut fine figures compared to a couple of simple cowpokes." Brazos' rugged features shadowed. "You know they ain't for us, don't you, Yank? When we leave here they'll go back to Stacey and Curly. Gals like them want somethin' they can hang onto."

"Why, Johnny Reb, I do believe you're sounding a little world-weary. Surely that's my style?"

Brazos looked wistfully across the yard. "It'd be kinda nice to settle down some place long enough for folks to get tired of the sight of your ugly mug, don't you reckon?"

"You'll never last that long, mister. Oh, I know you like to talk about owning your own spread and sleeping in the same bed every night—-but you will never make it, Reb, any more than I will. Like it or not, the die is cast for us. We've seen too much and done too much—and we know there's infinitely more to be seen and done. The next trail, the next town, the next pretty woman—in short, the unknown …"

9

Killer From the South

THE solitary horseman who came out of the timbered country high above the Fifty-four valley rode like a man familiar with the terrain. He didn't pause when he came to the granite cliffs that cut directly into the valley but simply guided his horse to the narrow cleft that even some of the ranch hands didn't know about, then he followed it down.

The gusty wind blowing off the rangeland tumbled his shoulder-length blond hair and hummed along the brim of his low-crowned hat. His shirt was of vivid red silk, unbuttoned to let the breeze at his lean body. The silk shirt, the eyepatch and the thonged-down Peacemaker Colt were the trappings by which men had come to know Kid Silk.

He rode into the valley and followed it north. A mile later he drew up in the shade of a cottonwood to look down the hill slope at the three men who worked on a small corral below.

After a while, he kneed the horse out of the shade and rode lazily towards them. He was halfway there before they sighted him. They promptly dropped the railing they were fitting into place and grabbed guns.

Kid Silk lifted a hand and called, "Take it easy, gents. I'm a friend."

The Fifty-four men were not prepared to take him at his word. Al Stock jacked a shell into his rifle chamber and said, "Get shuck of that hogleg of yours afore you come on, stranger."

Silk dropped his hands and kept riding. He made no move to lift his Colt.

"Don't be unsociable, boys," he called. "I'm here to see Joe Tucker. He's expectin' me."

Stock made a nervous movement with his rifle. The man in the red shirt looked dangerous. He could only be a gunslinger, and the Fifty-four men had seen too much of that kind of late to treat them lightly.

The hands were still indecisive when Silk reached them and drew rein. "Put 'em down, boys," he said quietly. "I could have gunned down the three of you and been on my way home for supper before you knew what hit you if I had been of a mind."

The lithe-hipped gunfighter watched as the guns were slowly lowered. He searched the faces of the three and only the weathered and leathered features of broken-down old Grampie Gunn struck a memory chord. But Grampie just stared at him, big-eyed, as if half expecting trouble.

"Go tell the boss-man I want to see him, boys," he murmured, stepping down, "I'll wait for him here."

Stock's hand shook a little on the rifle as he watched the stranger loop his reins over a post. "Who will I say wants to see him, mister?"

"Just tell him the Kid is here."

"The Kid?"

"Right."

Stock swallowed and turned to Tanner and Gunn. "I'll go to the house. You fellers better stay here."

"Mebbe I should go with you, Al," said young Billy Tanner. Billy had been cool enough before the man in the red shirt had appeared, but he perspired freely now.

"Glory!" Grampie Gunn said thinly. "If you boys think I'm gonna stay out here on my own with this—"

"The three of you go fetch Tucker," Kid Silk suggested, and even when he spoke in an easy, friendly way there was something in his voice that carried enormous weight. He limped to a pile of fence railings and sat down with his hat canted low over his lean face. He stretched out his stiff leg before him and rubbed his knee, staring east at the Three Buttes. He didn't glance their way when he spoke again. "Better move along now …"

The Fifty-four trio exchanged looks and then hurried to their horses. Once he was a distance from the figure on the railing pile, Al Stock called:

"You just stay put and don't try nothin' fancy, feller!"

Kid Silk didn't seem to hear. Dust clouds drifted past him as the horsemen started off. When they had gone, the gunfighter leaned back and rubbed his side against a frame post. Beneath the expensive silk shirt the gunman's post-straight back was crisscrossed with old scars. They still caused him discomfort from time to time, and silk was the only material that didn't irritate the twisted, puckered skin. His back was itching now. Badly.

***

The sheriff was on his way to the Mid-Town Diner late in the afternoon when he spotted Hank Brazos' dog squatted in the doorway of Watson's store. The fat lawman halted in the street, then changed direction to mount the store porch.

"Good day, old feller," he greeted the dog amiably and made to step past.

Bullpup bared his teeth. The sheriff stopped awkwardly.

"Now see here, dog," he said with authority, "you just cut out that face-pullin' and move aside."

Bullpup's hackles rose like the hump of a razorback hog. He wasn't always this belligerent, but his campaign against Curway Masters Vivian the Fourth had gone badly and so his temper these days was edgy. That bull might think he had his number at the moment, but he was not about to concede the same for any fat sheriff.

He barked and a familiar voice came from the gloomy interior.

"Cut that out, ugly!"

The sheriff was about to call to the unseen Brazos when steps sounded behind him. He turned to see Duke Benedict approaching, resplendent in black broadcloth and white linen, with a gold watch chain stretched across the flashy bed-of-flowers vest.

"Good afternoon, Sheriff Rudkin," Benedict greeted.

"Howdy there, Duke." Rudkin moved back from the door. "Just spotted the dog here and reckoned the Texan'd be about. Wanted to have a word with him about how things are goin' out on the spread, but that critter wouldn't budge out of the way."

"Never expect good manners from a cretin, Sheriff," Benedict drawled.

"That is an adage that often enables me to overlook the gaucheries of both that animal and its master." The gambling man smiled. "You'll be happy to know that everything is peaceful out at the ranch, Sheriff, so much so that Brazos and I were able to come to town to do a little shopping for tomorrow night's ball."

Rudkin answered Benedict's smile as he leaned a pudgy hand against an upright. "Well, that's good to hear, Duke. I figured Joe Tucker would be sensible enough to pull his horns in, but of course a man can't ever be sure." The sheriff paused to watch a wagon laden with timber roll by. Then he asked quietly, "Mr. Kincaid happy with the way things are goin'?"

"Any reason why he shouldn't be, Sheriff?"

Rudkin looked at Benedict levelly. "It's just that … well, I guess I've always had the feelin' that if one of them stiff-necked cattlemen ever got on top of the other, he'd be tempted to press home the advantage. No sign that Kincaid wants to do that, huh?"

Benedict shook his head. Two pretty girls came by, smiling and talking. They broke off when they saw Benedict and stared at him with undisguised interest. He doffed his hat and smiled. They halted.

"Will you be attending the ball tomorrow night, Mr. Benedict?" one asked boldly.

"Only if I have the assurance that you shall be there, fair lady."

The girl blushed. "Of course I shall be." She giggled as she took her companion's arm, and as they moved away the second girl looked back over her shoulder and dropped him a wink.

The sheriff shook his head in wonder. "Must be terrible to have womenfolk carry on about you that way, Duke."

"It's hell, Sheriff," Benedict said with a sigh, replacing his hat. Then he turned as Brazos appeared carrying a parcel wrapped in brown paper.

"They weren't out of stock?" Benedict asked, disappointed.

Brazos grinned amiably at Rudkin. "Nope, one purple shirt, largest size. How are things, Sheriff?"

"Well, just fine after what Duke's been tellin' me about things on the Anvil," Rudkin said. He looked from one to the other. "Lookin' forward to the ball, huh?"

"I should smile," Brazos replied. "You'll be there, Sheriff?"

"Yeah, I'll be there," Rudkin said without enthusiasm. "With my wife."

The sheriff's wife was ninety-five pounds of never-ending criticism. As the housing for her sharp tongue was scarcely glamorous, the lawman didn't anticipate too many men getting his wife up to dance, which meant he would be spending most of the evening twirling around with her himself and being told, "Don't step on my toes, Bernard," and "Straighten your back, Bernard, don't slump."

"You sound like a fellow who might need a little priming before the event, Sheriff," Benedict smiled.

"Speakin' of primin'," put in Brazos, "me and Benedict are goin' to have a quick one at the Silver Dollar afore headin' back to Anvil. Care to join us, Sheriff?"

"Don't mind if I do," Rudkin replied. Then, as they started off, the sheriff found himself studying Benedict from the corner of his eye. He was almost as tall as Duke Benedict, and only some ten years older. He wondered, if he trimmed off a hundred pounds and invested in a ninety-dollar suit and a flash vest, would Johnnie Lockyer and Maisie Brown start winking at him on the street?

Then, reflecting glumly on how his Harriet carried on if even some ancient biddy as much as looked his way, he decided it would be safer to pass up the glamour and continue to enjoy his food.

***

It was dusk when Joe Tucker appeared atop the grassy brown hill above the corral. Kid Silk limped slowly to and fro before the pens, his shirt the color of blood in the dying light. The big cattleman checked his horse and sat the saddle, a heavy, gray-garbed figure.

Silk halted and gazed up at the rancher. In the hills, coyotes began to call at the approach of night. A breeze stirred the long grass and flapped the brim of Tucker's old hat as he started down.

Silk waited with his back against the corral fence. "Tucker," he murmured as the rancher reined in before him.

"How'd you know I'm Tucker?" the big man asked. Tucker couldn't keep a certain brusqueness out of his voice. He had never liked this kind and his experience with the Brand brothers had given him no cause to alter his attitude.

"I know." Silk reached up and smoothed down his heavy, drooping moustache. "Step down, Tucker. I don't like talking up to a man."

Tucker hesitated for a moment, then dismounted. His eyes bored at the sleek gunslinger as he knotted the reins to a railing.

"You got my wire then?" Tucker grunted.

"Right."

"Why did you contact me?"

"You need help, don't you? You lost your guns, and Kincaid's got this Brazos and Benedict ridin' tall over there. What did you aim to do, just lay down and play dead?"

Joe Tucker's head canted to one side now as he studied the man with greater intensity. He let his eyes travel over the slender physique slowly, then fixed his stare on the lean, taut face. Tucker rubbed his jaw, his eyes down to slits.

"Do I know you from some place, Silk?"

The gunslinger smiled. "It's possible, Joe, quite possible …" The voice and the smile faded and Joe Tucker saw something like pain cut into the man's face. Kid Silk licked his lips. "Tell me, Joe, how is Cass keepin'?"

Joe Tucker felt a chill touch his flesh. "Cass?" he breathed. "Why should you be interested in my—"

He broke off abruptly. Kid Silk had suddenly pulled off his hat. His forehead was high and the thick fair hair curved back from it in heavy waves.

Joe Tucker felt his jaw fall open. *"You!"*

"*Me*, Joe."

***

By noon on Saturday it was already plain that there would be a record crowd at the ball. Ranchers and cowboys from the outlying spreads began arriving in force in the morning and by noon the Silver Dollar and Paylode Saloons were doing roaring business.

The ball marked the end of the spring roundup, but nobody was in much doubt as to why the dance this year was attracting so many people. The Anvil-Fifty-four feud which had cast its long shadow over Keogh County seemed to have ended. Sheridan was at last able to let its hair down and enjoy itself without the old tensions and enmities that had been part of the town's daily life for so long. Tonight would make up for a great deal for what they had suffered in the past, they told each other. It might well be the best night Sheridan had ever had.

The Anvil party arrived in town at dark, with the Kincaids in their big surrey, and Brazos, Benedict and the hands—apart from those left behind to guard the spread—flanking the carriage in a slicked-up and high-spirited cavalcade.

The dancing had already begun at the City Hall, but it was unanimously decided that everyone should take a drink at the hotel first.

Their appearance at the hotel caused a flurry, for Duke Benedict and Hank Brazos were considered to be the heroes of the day, and Emma Kincaid, lovely in a stunning green taffeta dress, was the loveliest girl in town tonight. Even Sarah looked pretty, everyone noted with surprise, and many an envious glance was directed her way by the women present when they saw the way the handsome Duke Benedict danced attention upon her. Stacey Blaine was there, too, looking uncomfortable in a store-bought shirt and new moleskins but it was plain that Sarah had eyes only for Benedict.

And then there was Brazos' new shirt. The comments, as the towering Texan hustled to the bar to get Emma a sarsaparilla, ranged from "Color-ful" to "I should have brought my smoked glasses tonight."

Hank Brazos thought he looked just right. He had even polished up his range boots and gunbelt, proof of how important he regarded this occasion. He had also given Bullpup a bath, an event that had filled the air around the Anvil headquarters with pitiful howls of protest during the afternoon. Scrubbed, brushed and trimmed to within an inch of his life, Bullpup was strangely meek and lethargic, obviously aware that his rugged image had been tarnished, perhaps beyond redemption.

"Wind is risin' some," Curly Calem announced when they had finished their drinks. "Better get along to the hall so the girls don't get all dusted up."

There was an awkward moment as they started for the doors and Joe Tucker and his daughter came in with several Fifty-four riders. People were astonished to see how tired and grim Tucker looked. He hadn't been seen in town for a week, and it looked as if it had been a hard week indeed for the boss of Fifty-four. His daughter, grave and thin in a simple blue gown, nodded to the Kincaid girls but stared at their father as if he were a stranger. Emma and Sarah spoke to Cass and Tucker. The rancher tried to smile, but it didn't quite come off. As the Anvil party walked by, a few standing close saw Joe Tucker lift his hand towards Duke Benedict as if he were about to speak. But he didn't catch Benedict's eye, and he let his hand drop, then led his daughter deeper into the lobby.

Tucker was forgotten when the Anvil party reached the hall. The band struck up a lively tune and Brazos and Benedict were obliged to move fast to claim the girls ahead of a concerted rush from the stag line. Burk Kincaid made his way to the official dais where the mayor sat with his wife, flanked by Sheriff and Mrs. Rudkin and other notables. The Anvil hands descended on the girls lining the walls. Those who failed to secure partners shrugged philosophically and headed for the bar.

Before the first hour had passed, everybody agreed that the night had exceeded even the highest expectations. The music pumped out by the Sheridan Country Band was far above their normal standard and there was excitement in the very air.

Familiar faces looking unfamiliar over winged collars and strange ties … suits with the mothball smell still strong on them but brushed and pressed to elegance … perfume and the tinkling sound of women's laughter … bare arms and snowy shoulders with stones and pearls glittering beneath the lights … songs and happy voices … all blending in a shifting panorama of color and sound …

They were all there tonight. Mayor Snipes, thin and mustached, danced with his enormous wife and ogled the girls. Jackson Krebbs of the Paylode, exhibiting his most garish waistcoat, partnered one of his percentage girls, a statuesque brunette named Carrielle who did things to a waltz that would have brought whistles from the men present but for the inhibiting presence of their wives. Joe Slater of Slater's store; Brick Farraday of the Gunsight ranch with his wife who was twenty years younger; hands from the Anvil, the Fifty-four and other ranches as far as fifty miles away. Everybody was there having a marvelous time—but Duke Benedict was quite certain he was having the best time of all.

Dancing in turn with Sarah, Emma and the pretty girls who had accosted him on the street the previous day, Benedict found himself in the happy position of having women come up to him to book dances.

The more he danced and gave himself over to the full-hearted enjoyment of the night, the more distant seemed the violence of the past weeks. The shootout with the Brands had depressed him far more than it had Brazos, who seemed to have the happy knack of shutting such things from his mind, and he realized now that Brazos had been right in insisting that they attend the ball. A man needed something like this to ease the tensions out of him, and Benedict was feeling so chipper that he was actually considering going to Rudkin's aid by asking his mean-lipped wife to dance, when Curly Calem entered the hall to tell him there was a man outside who wanted to see him.

"Who is it?" Benedict asked. He was talking to Emma and Sarah near the punch bowl at the time.

"He didn't say, Duke," Curly replied. "But I don't like the cut of his rig."

It was only then, as he looked at Calem, that Benedict realized the man had gone pale. Benedict frowned.

"What does he look like, Curly?"

Curly Calem swallowed. "I guess ..." he paused to glance at the girls, "... I guess he looks like a gunslinger, Duke."

A faint bell rang in Benedict's head, like the sound of old dangers remembered. Sarah brought a hand to her breasts and Emma gasped. Then Curly Calem added:

"I asked him why he wanted to see you, Duke, but he told me it wasn't his night to talk to the small-timers. He said he was in the frame of mind to talk with somebody ... real big."

"Duke," Sarah said, "don't go out."

Benedict looked over the heads at the doors, feeling remote, a cold current running through him. Brazos, standing nearby, caught his look. The Texan frowned, then excused himself to Barney Rudkin and crossed to the table.

"What's the matter, Yank?" Brazos asked. "You're lookin' right peaked."

"There's a pilgrim out in the street by Slater's store who says he wants to see Duke, Hank," Curly Calem said. "Looks like trouble."

"The hell you say," Brazos breathed. Then: "Look, you stay here, Yank. I'll go take a gander at this feller and—"

"No," Benedict said. "This fellow wants to see me …"

"Then by Judas I'm comin' with you."

Sarah grasped Benedict's arm and he touched her hand lightly. Then he went to the doors just as the Sheridan Country Band struck up *Turkey In The Straw*.

10

The Last Gunfight

K ID SILK stood in the shadowy street in front of Slater's store. Thin gusts of wind fluttered the full sleeves of his shirt that was the color of blood. He didn't move as Benedict and Brazos emerged from the brightly lit hall across the street, followed by a stream of men, with here and there the odd bright flash of a woman's dress among the crowd. He watched with his one bright eye as the gunfighters halted to motion the people back before starting slowly across the street towards him.

Then the Kid lifted a hand. "Just you, Benedict! For starters, that is! With luck, I won't need to do business with the Texan."

Brazos and Benedict halted.

"Stay put, Johnny Reb," Benedict murmured. "I can—"

"Never mind that, Benedict," Brazos said harshly. "This ain't no fool game, amigo. If that jasper is lookin' for trouble, then we'll give it to him double."

"I'm afraid he's above your class, Brazos."

"Now how in the name of all that's holy do you reckon you can tell *that* just by lookin'?"

The gambling man's handsome face turned bitter. "It's one of the very few advantages of reaching my status in this bloody business, Reb. You get so you can always tell—just by looking."

"But—"

"Stay put!" Benedict snapped. "If he can kill me, he'll butcher you

95

like a hog. So if it comes to gun smoke and I can't defeat him, then you back water, Texan. You're always telling me not to be a hero—well, now is the time to take your own advice."

Benedict moved on then, leaving Hank Brazos staring after him with a feeling of helplessness.

The word that trouble was afoot had swept through the hall in a minute and the crowd was now pouring into the street on a great wave of sound. But Benedict barely heard.

His every instinct was channeled into a tight track now, and his every nerve was fined down as he strode closer to the lithe figure in the crimson silk shirt.

The man lifted his hand. "Close enough, Benedict—for talking or anything else. And it could be that all we'll do is talk."

"Who are you, mister?"

"They call me Kid Silk."

There was a concerted gasp from the crowd. Kid Silk, the border killer!

But if Duke Benedict was impressed, none of it showed in his voice as he said, "You have business with me, Kid?"

"I've come to ask you and the Texan to leave Anvil."

"Why?"

"I have reasons."

"You'll have to spell them out, I'm afraid."

"Don't want to."

Benedict lifted his chin. "Did Tucker hire you?"

"Not exactly. I offered to help him out, gratis."

"Why? My experience with your kind is that you do nothing for nothing."

The breeze tugged at Kid Silk's thick moustache. The gunfighter smoothed it down with his long fingers. "Joe Tucker told me that you were kind of sharp-tongued, Benedict, and I see that it's so. I suppose at another time I might enjoy cutting you down to size, but not the way things are. You see, from what Joe told me, Benedict, I reckon that you and Brazos are all right. In truth, Joe wasn't all that anxious for me to buy in, but I kind of persuaded him that it was for the best. I've got nothing personal against you fellers, except that you're riding for the wrong brand."

"In your opinion."

"It's true, Benedict. Believe me, I know." Here a note of emotion crept into Kid Silk's voice for the first time. "Kincaid started this feud and only he kept it going, friend. It's not for you to know why. But I know, and I'm telling you it just isn't right that Kincaid should get on top of the Fifty-four this way. Joe deserves a chance, and the only way he'll get it is if you two fellers leave. So that's it, friend. Just tell me that you and Brazos will pack your traps and leave Joe and Kincaid free to work things out for themselves, then the two of us can go have a drink together."

Benedict shook his head. "I'm sorry, but I can't do that. We've had to kill to achieve this peace, Kid. And some of our men were killed. If we walked out, it would mean those men died for nothing. I couldn't live with that."

"Then I'll have to kill you."

"Not necessarily. It isn't too late for you to back away. Kid."

"Sorry."

Benedict nodded slowly. "So am I ... very sorry."

Kid Silk shifted his weight. "I wish you hadn't put me to this, Benedict, but make your play."

"If that's the only way ..."

"It's the only way now."

Time seemed to hang suspended for long seconds. Then both men moved together. Guns came out together, and two men who didn't know what it was like to be bettered, triggered as one. Gun-crashes rolled down the street and gun smoke billowed and was snatched away by the breeze. There were only two shots, and when the echoes had died, Benedict and Kid Silk still stood facing each other. Then Kid Silk took one faltering step and fell forward on his face.

The crowd started forward, but Benedict reached the fallen man first. He knelt and turned him over. There was dust on Kid Silk's face and blood ran from his mouth. His eye was a brilliant, feverish.

"I thought I could beat you, Benedict."

"It's a chancy business, Kid—you know that."

"But ... but I wanted to beat you ... to bring *him* down."

"Who?"

The crowd was around them now. Kid Silk's dimming eye scanned their faces. "Him!" he said, and he still had the strength to snarl.

He was staring directly at Burk Kincaid.

Benedict looked up at Kincaid who was flanked by his daughters and Hank Brazos. Then he turned his puzzled gaze back to the dying gunfighter.

"Why, Kid? What was your grudge against Kincaid?"

"Grudge?" Silk panted, his glazed eye still on Kincaid. *"You* know it was more than a grudge, don't you, old man? I ... I waited a long time to come back. I could have come back any time ... but I figured Joe would even the account in the end. When ... when he looked like losin' out, I knew it was time to come home and help even things up ... for what you did to me and Cass ..."

There was something extra in the air now, some terrible mystery. Burk Kincaid stepped closer. His mouth was open in horror but no sound came from his lips. Suddenly Cass Tucker was there, throwing herself down on her knees at Kid Silk's side. The dying man managed a smile for Tucker's daughter. "Sorry, Cass—for everything." Then his head rolled and he was dead.

"Virgil!" Cass Tucker's scream went down the spines of the onlookers like a whipsaw blade.

"It can't be!" Burk Kincaid cried hoarsely. He brushed the girl aside and ripped at the dead man's shirt. The silk tore away, revealing the old whip scars.

"Virgil," Kincaid muttered brokenly. "My boy is dead."

***

"He talked me into it," Joe Tucker said in a dead monotone. "I'd ... I'd had my fill of the whole dirty business and wanted it ended. But I was afraid Kincaid would strike again the way he did so often afore, and when Virgil promised he'd try to get rid of Brazos and Benedict without gunplay ... I just weakened and gave in."

The men sat around the polished table in the Sheridan Council Chambers staring at Joe Tucker—Duke Benedict, Hank Brazos, General Madison, Sheriff Rudkin and Burk Kincaid. It was late afternoon on the day after Kid Silk's death. With Indian renegade, Many Kills in chains,

Madison had been on his way back to Fort Hook via Sheridan when news of the gunfight reached him by telegraph at Parnell. The general and ten troopers had made a forced ride ahead of the main force to reach Sheridan, where Madison had promptly summoned Tucker and the Anvil men.

Tucker and Kincaid had been at their respective outfits when the troopers arrived with Madison's message. Sheridan had anticipated a fresh outbreak of Fifty-four-Anvil violence following the gunfight in the street, but it hadn't eventuated, for Joe Tucker had left town immediately after the fight, while Burk Kincaid seemed to have lapsed into deep shock. Dr. Perry had administered a strong sedative to Kincaid before allowing his daughters and hands to take him home.

General Madison didn't know that Curly Calem and Stacey Blaine had had to dress Burk Kincaid before Benedict and Brazos could drive him in in the surrey. As they sat in silence now, Kincaid's attention was caught by a droning fly. He followed it with rapt attention, as if the fly were the most significant object in the room.

Unaware of Kincaid's distraction, Madison grimaced as the smoke from Benedict's cigar wafted past his face, then he spoke brusquely to Tucker:

"Let me have it all, so that I may make a decision, Mr. Tucker. And I mean all of it."

Tucker sighed, and Brazos and Benedict leaned forward intently to hear his words, for there were still huge gaps in their knowledge of Virgil Kincaid and the events that had brought him to Sheridan with his gun.

"It was all over my daughter," Tucker said in the same dead voice. "Around five years ago, she and Virgil started seein' one another on the quiet. They fell in love. After a couple of months, Kincaid got wind of it. He went loco. He'd always looked down his nose at me and he wasn't gonna have no son of his gettin' mixed up with the daughter of a man he hated."

Tucker paused to stare at the expressionless Kincaid, then went on:

"The night Kincaid found out, he braced Virgil and told him he wasn't to see Cass no more. Virgil refused, so Kincaid took a whip to him to show he meant it. I guess he lost his temper, on account of he lashed the kid up somethin' fierce. Now Virge was always mighty wild, and what happened to him that night must've pushed him over the edge. He told

99

me out on my place when he came Friday that a couple of days after he quit Anvil, he got drunk down in Toonerville, got into a ruckus and shot a man. Turned out this jasper was a gunnie of some note, with two brothers. The brothers come after Virge and he shot them down, too. Word got around there was a new gun packer. Afore he knew it, there were kids comin' after his scalp and he was cuttin' 'em down. He got his face on wanted dodgers all over, so after a while the only work he could get was with a Colt."

"Yes, the fellow did that indeed," Madison said. "There was a time when I assigned five troopers to hunt Kid Silk down, but I have the suspicion that they didn't try too hard." The general looked speculatively at Benedict. "Kid Silk was considered unbeatable in some quarters."

"No man is unbeatable," Benedict murmured, then he glanced at Tucker. "It's still not clear why Virgil came back here, Joe."

"He hated his father somethin' fierce," Tucker explained. "He held Kincaid responsible for turnin' him into a gunman. Virge was full of hate and pain when he left Keogh County, and by the time he calmed down some he was wearin' a big reputation they forced him to live up to. And bein' a killer for hire, he knew he couldn't come back for Cass. He never stopped lovin' her, he said … loved her too much to saddle her with his bloody name …"

Silence fell in the room again as they digested the tragic story of Virgil Kincaid. Then Madison said:

"What you are saying, Tucker, is that Virgil elected to come back when he heard of your reverses, just so his father wouldn't win the infernal range war?"

"That's it, General." Tucker got up and walked to the window. "I guess I did wrong, lettin' him talk me into standin' against Duke. If I've got punishment comin', then I'm ready to take it. But if I was to fetch ten years, I'd say at the end of it what I'll say now—I was scared of Kincaid and always have been—that's what made me agree to Virge comin' in. I never wanted the fight to go on, but Kincaid wouldn't let me quit. Every time I tried he'd start it up again."

He turned and faced them.

"You see, that was why Kincaid came to hate me so hard, too—him and Virge. Virge held his father responsible for ruinin' his life, and in turn Kincaid held me responsible for losin' his son. They were both eaten up by hate. Now that hate has killed one of 'em—and it's damn nigh done for the other by the look of it."

Brazos studied Kincaid, then he turned to Benedict. "What do you say, Yank? Does Tucker's story hold water with you?"

Benedict nodded slowly. "Yes, it does, mainly because it answers all the mysteries and questions I couldn't shape answers to before." He sat pensively for a long while before looking up. "General, I know the final decision here rests with you. You were disappointed here before when you thought matters had come to an end, and I couldn't blame you for being skeptical now. But I honestly believe that it is finally over, and that you'd do best by not thinking of guilt or punishment. Let the past be buried and let the county get on with the business of living again."

"That's all very well—if we can be assured of the goodwill of both parties, sir," Madison replied crisply.

"Well, you've got my goodwill, for one, General," Tucker insisted. "I got me a daughter out at my place who won't ever get over what happened here, and all this feudin' and fightin' has nigh run me broke. I can tell you here and now that I'm through with battlin' the Anvil. I'm ready to make any sort of peace you want. And if it starts again, then I'll sell up and move out. I can let you have that in writin' if you want."

The general was impressed. It was true that Tucker was at least partly responsible for the latest violence, but now, as before, it was difficult to sheet home the blame to any quarter. Madison studied the Fifty-four man for a long moment, then he turned his attention to Burk Kincaid.

"How about you, Mr. Kincaid? Are you willing to give me an assurance of good intent?"

Kincaid looked at him with blank eyes. "Pardon?"

"The gen'l wants to know if you'll bury the hatchet with Tucker, Mr. Kincaid," Brazos said gently.

"Tucker?" Kincaid said vaguely. "Oh, yes … yes, of course. I agree. I wouldn't want anything to happen to my boy …"

"Your boy, sir?" Madison snapped. "Your boy is—"

He broke off at Benedict's warning gesture.

Duke said, "Will you shake hands with Tucker, Mr. Kincaid? You refused before, but I believe it's time now."

"Yes, of course. High time, Mr. Benedict," Kincaid said quickly. He smiled brightly at Tucker. "Virgil has always spoken highly of you, Joe, and I respect his opinion. A fine, smart boy that, Joe. A man has no worries about how things will be after he's gone with a lad like that at the helm. Too bad you never had a son, Joe, but …"

Kincaid suddenly fell silent, confusion spreading over his face. It was pitiful to see. The deep-set eyes, so clear and positive there for a few moments, wandered around the room. After a while he rose from his chair and picked up his hat, each movement preceded by a pause. The onlookers could almost hear the whir and click of some vital mechanism gone wrong.

When he had his hat on his head, he stood indecisively, blinking at Tucker as he approached.

Sadness showed in Joe Tucker's heavy face as he extended his hand. Kincaid looked down at the hand, then grabbed it and pumped it vigorously. A single tear ran down his cheek.

So ended the Keogh County range war.

***

They were quiet days on Anvil. Duke Benedict and Hank Brazos knew they should leave, but they seemed to be waiting for some signal to tell them it was time.

That afternoon they had ridden out to the border with Stacey Blaine and Curly Calem. They had sighted a group of Fifty-four cowhands and had been invited across to their line camp for coffee. Stacey Blaine and Fifty-four ramrod Shep Beckett had talked about turning the broad graze area around Three Buttes into common winter range for steers from both outfits. Blaine had assured Beckett the plan would definitely be implemented before they parted. Stacey was in a position to make decisions on the Anvil now, for the operation of the spread had passed into the hands of the foreman and the Kincaid girls.

Blaine was up at the house. The ramrod had been invited for supper, but Brazos and Benedict were not included in the invitation. The pair were still on good terms with the sisters, but it wasn't the same. Duke Benedict had killed their brother. Both Emma and Sarah insisted that it made no difference to their attitudes, but the two tall men knew better. A dead boy stood between them and two young girls, and always would.

Benedict smoke a cigar, Brazos a brown-paper cigarette. Their thoughts ran deep as they gazed up at the great house that harbored a broken man.

Locked in their thoughts, they were slow to grow aware of the great racket from the stud bull's pen over the knoll.

As hands came running into the yard to stare, the great challenging roar of Stinker washed over the headquarters, punctuated by Bullpup's battle cry. Then came a splintering crash, a howl of pain, and a rising cloud of dust.

Brazos shook his head wearily. "I better go get the liniment ready."

"A gun," Benedict said. "It would be cheaper in the end, Johnny Reb, and a lot more satisfactory."

Brazos just grunted and started across the yard, then he propped when he glimpsed a black-and-white spotted streak burst across the knoll and headed towards headquarters.

Bullpup came on at full notch with something flopping from his jaws. Everybody thought it was a strip of dark-colored cloth at first, before their attention was distracted from the dog by the sight of Curway Masters Vivian. With splinters of a battered pen rail hanging to his coat, the great bull loomed free and furious over the crest and came thundering down after the bounding dog.

Alarm spread through the yard and men jumped for cover. Brazos hesitated until the enraged bull sideswiped a heavy gatepost and sent it flying end over end, then he too dashed for the stables.

Bullpup zoomed into the yard. His ugly mouth was twisted high at the corners in a grin of evil triumph around his length of flopping rag. But it wasn't a flopping rag, the horrified spectators realized as he dashed towards the bunkhouse. It was the last foot of Curway Masters Vivian the Fourth's aristocratic tail.

Probably drunk with triumph, Bullpup elected to scamper into the bunkhouse instead of attempting to outrun his enemy.

The bunkhouse proved a costly choice of a sanctuary.

Curway Masters Vivian charged straight for the building's main entrance despite the fact that it wasn't wide enough for his huge, red-backed bulk. Door frames splintered and the entire building shook as he crashed through.

The first thing the bull saw inside was Tolliver Trane. Tolliver had been resting on his bunk at the end of a hard day when the clamor awakened him. He got sleepily to his feet and stood near his bunk blearily hooking up his suspenders when more than a thousand pounds of dynamite thundered in.

Tolliver blinked in alarm. The next moment he hurtled fifteen feet through the air to land unhurt but mighty surprised on a bunk that fell to pieces beneath him.

The bull ignored the man as he clattered the length of the bunkhouse leaving vast destruction in his wake.

Bullpup had taken refuge in the gear room at the western end of the bunkhouse. Observing the bull coming towards the room at high speed, he bounded onto a bed and leaped for a window. Stinker charged the door. It was narrower and more substantial than the front door which he had demolished. His head and withers got through, but the mighty shoulders stuck. The air trembled to his bellowing as he first tried to force his way in, and when this failed, tried to back out.

He found he could do neither. He was stuck fast, yet even so it took every man on the place with twenty ropes to finally free him and drag him back to the corral where he was roped to a snubbing post while repairs were effected.

With his hat canted over one eye and coated from head to toe with dust, a dazed Hank Brazos backed away from the still fighting stud bull and looked at Benedict. He fully expected a rich flood of wrath to flow over him, but to his astonishment the gambling man looked calm enough as he leaned against the corral fence smoking a cigar.

He soon discovered why.

"I rather feel we have been waiting for something to get us moving, Johnny Reb," Benedict drawled. "I sense the signal, and the time, have come."

The Texan could only pant, "Time? Man, I reckon it's *high* time!"

***

Stars shone down brightly from a clear Nevada sky as they rode out. Figures waved from the yard when their horses climbed the knoll beyond the bunkhouse. Emma had cried and Sarah had insisted that Duke write to her, but neither Duke Benedict nor Hank Brazos put much store in the touching farewells. They had seen, with eyes wise in such matters, that Sarah and Emma were secretly relieved to see them go. They rode too tall, stepped too heavy, and cut too wide a swathe to be comfortable with. In the long term, solid, hard-working fellows like Stacey Blaine and Curly Calem were best for good girls.

Most likely Stacey and Curly would remember them longer and more clearly, Benedict thought hopefully as they rode. Their handshakes had been firm and strong, and their parting words had carried depth. Being men, Blaine and Calem would more clearly understand the enormous weight Brazos and Benedict had had to carry here; they could even understand that when hatreds burned as they had here in Keogh County, it was the gun and only the gun that could put out the fires.

The trail partners struck west, crossed the Fifty-four border and rode for the high country. From a ridge they saw the distant lights of Joe Tucker's house.

When the lights had vanished, Brazos took up his harmonica and blew a tune through it. And the wind blew sweet and gentle from the south.

THE END

ABOUT THE AUTHOR

E. Jefferson Clay was just one of many pseudonyms used by New South Wales-born **Paul Wheelahan** (1930-2018). Starting off as a comic-book writer/illustrator, Paul created *The Panther* and *The Raven* before moving on to a long and distinguished career as a western writer. Under the names Emerson Dodge, Brett McKinley, E. Jefferson Clay, Ben Jefferson and others, he penned more than 800 westerns  and could, at his height, turn out a full-length western in just four days.

The son of a mounted policeman, Paul initially worked as a powder monkey on the Oaky River Dam project. By 1955, however, he was drawing *Davy Crockett—Frontier Scout.* In 1963 he began his long association with Australian publisher Cleveland Pty. Co. Ltd. As prolific as he was as a western writer, however, he also managed to write for TV, creating shows like *Runaways* and contributing scripts to perennial favorites like *A Country Practice.*

At the time of his death, in December 2018, he was writing his auto-biography, *Never Ride Back* … which was also the title of his very first western.

BENEDICT AND BRAZOS

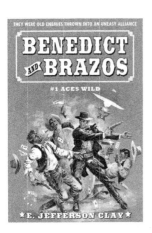

Aces Wild
Two brawling Civil War veterans join forces to recover $200,000 gold — for themselves!

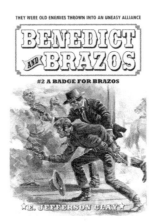

A Badge for Brazos
Harmony was a powder-keg of miners, ranchers and gun-toughs. Benedict and Brazos found every gun trained on them!

The Big Ranchero
Someone was rustling cattle at Rancho Antigua, and it might have been Bo Rangle! But where had the cattle gone?

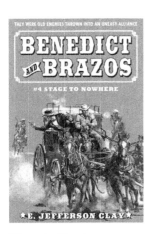

Stage to Nowhere
Jack Savage's gang attacked a stage carrying their leader to trial, leading to a standoff in a ghost town.

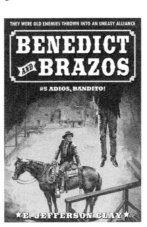

Adios, Bandido!
Race Sackett could lead Benedict and Brazos to Bo Rangle — but only if they could rescue him from a deserving noose.

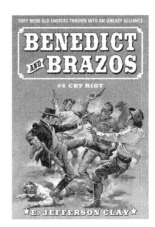

Cry Riot
Foley Kingston asked Benedict to break the miners' strike — but Brazos wondered if they were on the right side.

BENEDICT AND BRAZOS

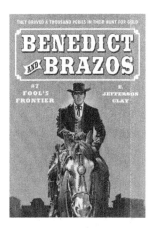

Fool's Frontier
While Benedict and Brazos are guests of a religious order, a criminal gang arrives to reclaim the town.

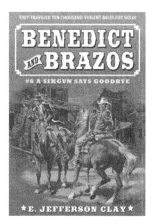

A Sixgun Says Goodbye
Brazos' old commanding officer is kidnapped and held for a ransom his lovely daughter can't possibly raise.

The Living Legend
Benedict pins on a badge to crush the Yellow House gang, but their leader is his old gun-fighting mentor.

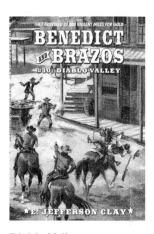

Diablo Valley
An intentional case of mistaken identity puts the hangman's noose on the wrong neck — and turns loose the real outlaw!

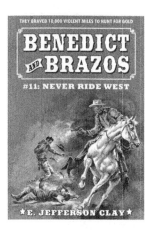

Never Ride West
Benedict and Brazos are are hired to bodyguard Governor Garfield — but who is the hidden assassin's *actual* target?

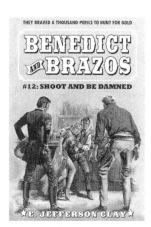

Shoot and Be Damned
The clock is ticking on the boys' best lead as outlaw Bo Rangle moves his hidden gold from one location to another.

Printed in Great Britain
by Amazon

44744651R00067